KU-742-608

'Were you chosen for your beauty and your sex-appeal, do you think?' Xavier asked, his dark eyes glittering.

'Of course I wasn't!' Laura defended. 'My sex-appeal is not only irrelevant but inappropriate in a country like Kharastan.'

'So it's just some kind of coincidence that they should have appointed a nubile young woman to do the job?' he questioned, his voice edgy with desire.

'I don't know,' she whispered, as if she had suddenly come to realise the trap she found herself in. Backed up against the wall, and ostensibly alone on a powerful jet with a powerful man whose whole large and muscular frame emanated a raw kind of sexuality.

'Don't you?' he whispered back, and touched the tip of his finger to her chin, tilting it upwards and forcing her to meet the piercing black gaze. 'I think you do. Just as I think that someone told the Sheikh's entourage about those rosebud lips and knew that I would want to

London Borough of Barking and Dagenham

90600000143741

THE DESERT PRINCES

by
Sharon Kendrick

Proud and passionate...

Three billionaires are soon to discover the truth
of their ancestry...

Wild and untamed...

They are all heirs to the throne of the
desert kingdom of Kharastan...
Though royalty is their destiny, these sheikhs
are as untamed as their homeland!

THE DESERT PRINCES

From the magnificent Blue Palace to the
wild plains of the desert, be swept away
as
three sheikh princes find their brides.

Coming soon

April 2007
THE SHEIKH'S UNWILLING WIFE

May 2007
THE DESERT KING'S VIRGIN BRIDE

THE SHEIKH'S ENGLISH BRIDE

BY
SHARON KENDRICK

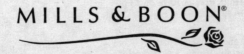
MILLS & BOON®

DID YOU PURCHASE THIS BOOK WITHOUT A COVER?

If you did, you should be aware it is **stolen property** as it was reported *unsold and destroyed* by a retailer. Neither the author nor the publisher has received any payment for this book.

All the characters in this book have no existence outside the imagination of the author, and have no relation whatsoever to anyone bearing the same name or names. They are not even distantly inspired by any individual known or unknown to the author, and all the incidents are pure invention.

All Rights Reserved including the right of reproduction in whole or in part in any form. This edition is published by arrangement with Harlequin Enterprises II B.V. The text of this publication or any part thereof may not be reproduced or transmitted in any form or by any means, electronic or mechanical, including photocopying, recording, storage in an information retrieval system, or otherwise, without the written permission of the publisher.

This book is sold subject to the condition that it shall not, by way of trade or otherwise, be lent, resold, hired out or otherwise circulated without the prior consent of the publisher in any form of binding or cover other than that in which it is published and without a similar condition including this condition being imposed on the subsequent purchaser.

MILLS & BOON and MILLS & BOON with the Rose Device are registered trademarks of the publisher.

First published in Great Britain 2007
Harlequin Mills & Boon Limited,
Eton House, 18-24 Paradise Road, Richmond, Surrey TW9 1SR

© Sharon Kendrick 2007

ISBN-13: 978 0 263 85301 8
ISBN-10:   0 263 85301 2

Set in Times Roman 10 ½ on 13 pt
01-0307-42785

Printed and bound in Spain
by Litografia Rosés, S.A., Barcelona

THE SHEIKH'S ENGLISH BRIDE

To Fiona (passenger) Hartley—

inspirational walking companion
and general *bonne amie*

CHAPTER ONE

XAVIER dangled the skimpy pair of panties from an out-stretched finger and raised a quizzical black brow at the pouting blonde.

'Aren't you forgetting something, *cherie*?' he murmured, in the outrageously sexy accent which some-times caused people to ask whether he did radio voice-overs in his spare time. The answer, of course, was no—Xavier de Maistre did not need to dabble in the media to supplement his already vast income.

Only once had he exploited his sensually beauti-ful dark face and muscularly hard body—when he had been talent-spotted as a teenager, walking down the Champs Elysées. He had been paid a fortune to ad-vertise an aftershave, but had astonished the world by turning down the many lucrative offers which had followed the campaign's massive success. Instead, he had taken the money and used it to found his property empire, which was now one of the biggest in the world.

The blonde parted her lips. 'Don't you want to play that game any more?' she questioned huskily.

Xavier's cool expression did not waver. Did she imagine that nothing had changed since their affair had ended last year, and that he would have stayed the same instead of moving on? That he was turned on by the fact that she had arrived—supposedly for coffee and a 'catch up'—and then left the most intimate item of her underwear in an exquisite heap on the polished floor of his Parisian apartment?

His mouth curved in derision. Ex-lovers could be so *boring*. Could anything be less of a turn-on than the thought of having sex with a woman you had tired of?

Yet, when she had telephoned him yesterday, he had readily agreed to a meeting. A year had elapsed, and so he had assumed they'd be able to have the civilised drink she'd suggested. But from the moment he had seen her—the expression in her eyes and the oh-so-obvious way she had sat squirming and drinking coffee—he had guessed what she wanted. He sighed. Some women just never let up

'I think we exhausted all the possibilities of that game a long time ago, don't you?' he replied evenly, his black eyes glinting. 'Nice try, *cherie*—but maybe you should replay it with a man who can appreciate you—as you should be appreciated.'

'Xavier—'

But he stayed her with a slight shake of the head. 'Didn't you say you had a plane to catch?'

Xavier could read the momentary indecision which flitted across her lovely face. She was wondering whether he was really turning down the opportunity to have sex. But she was also an intelligent woman, and maybe she recognised that there was no point. That some things were best left unsaid, and at least that way you left with your dignity intact.

So she shrugged and took the panties from him, and began to wriggle them on underneath her pure silk skirt—and at that moment Xavier's resolve wavered and he almost changed his mind.

It would have been ridiculously easy. There was a bedroom located at the far end of the corridor, with a large bed with crisp Egyptian cotton sheets and views right down to the River Seine.

Xavier owned the entire building, and it housed the offices of his empire—but he maintained a luxury apartment in the penthouse, hence the bedroom. The excuse he used was that sometimes his business deals went on through the night—he needed to have a place to sleep and he wasn't crazy about hotels.

It was well known in the city that he entertained his women there, and its presence only added to Xavier's legendary status as lover-extraordinaire. He was a man with a huge appetite for all the good things in life—and he had worked hard to get to just this place.

He turned to look out of the window, where the vast stretch of the river glittered and glimmered in the afternoon light.

From here he could see the boats which glided through the sleek waters, filled with awestruck tourists as they overdosed on the beautiful monuments which lined the river. But Paris had that effect on people. It was a city that infused his blood, his heart and his soul—a place which engaged him more than any woman ever could. He frowned, realising that he couldn't remember the last time he had made love.

So why turn down this opportunity? mocked a voice in his head.

Maybe because it *was* too easy. Xavier had never liked anything which came too easily—probably because nothing ever had.

'I don't suppose I'm ever going to see you again, am I, Xavier?'

The blonde's voice broke into his thoughts and his black eyes narrowed as he slowly turned around, acknowledging that her particular appeal had faded for ever and knowing that he shouldn't be surprised. It always happened. No matter how beautiful or accomplished his lovers, his appetite always grew jaded. Was it that once he had conquered them there seemed nothing left worth staying around for? A challenge, always a challenge—and, once conquered, there was always another just waiting...

'Who knows, *cherie*?' he murmured, with a lazy shrug of his shoulders. 'Sometimes I am lucky enough to travel to New York. Maybe we could have dinner next time I'm in town?'

They stared at one another, both knowing that this would be the last time they would meet. But what did she expect? She bit her lip. 'Sure. You're a bastard—do you know that?' she said softly.

'Am I?' he queried. Then the phone began to ring and he turned his back on her to answer it.

'*Oui?*'

He frowned as he listened to what his assistant was saying.

'I have someone down here who would like to see you, Xavier.'

Without an appointment? Xavier stilled, for he had an instinctive distrust of being taken by surprise. And what the hell did Security think they were playing at?

'Not another damned journalist?' he snapped—for the building had been practically under seige for a couple of weeks after France's biggest-selling weekly *Bonjour!* had published some snatched balcony photos. The pictures of Xavier sleepily buttoning up a pair of faded old jeans seemed to have found their way into the national consciousness, and women were downloading the images off the internet. Given the country's fierce privacy laws, the matter was currently in the hands of his lawyers.

'No, it's no one from the Press,' said his assistant.

'Well, who is it, and what does he want?' he snapped.

'It's a she, and she won't say. She says she wants to speak to you personally.'

'Oh, does she?' Xavier lowered his voice. 'Do I know her?'

'She says not.'

'I see.' Just the fact that his assistant had not kicked the unexpected stranger out spoke volumes. Xavier only employed people whose instincts he trusted, and he was always prepared to listen to them.

His gaze flickered over to the blonde, who was still staring at him with a sulky expression, and he wondered how the hell he was going to get rid of her. Maybe this unknown woman was a blessing in disguise—presenting him with a legitimate reason to seamlessly extricate himself from this awkward situation.

'Tell her to wait,' he said smoothly. 'I'll be down in a little while, when I have finished here.' He put the phone down.

The blonde turned on him and nodded her head slowly. 'You've got someone else. Of course you have. How stupid of me.' She gave a hollow laugh. 'Did I somehow imagine that you'd still be available a year later, maybe pining for me, and hoping we could pick up where we left off?'

A shadow passed over his dark face. 'I never promised you anything, Nancy. I didn't realise that there was going to be some kind of *problem*.'

'That's just the trouble,' she said softly. 'You create the problem because you're so damned *good*. Goodbye, Xavier—and thanks for the memory.' And she walked out of the room with her head held high.

Xavier's eyes narrowed into ebony slivers as he heard the elevator whirring into action to take her downstairs.

Had he acted dishonourably? No, he had not—to have been dishonourable he would have availed himself of her body today and then sent her on her way. He felt the ache of sexual frustration and knew that other men would think him a fool.

But Xavier was careful. He was fastidious in his choice of lovers, and he had only two rules when it came to making that choice: that they must be very beautiful and that there must be no deep emotional attachment or commitment. He made it clear very early on that he was neither interested in love nor marriage, for he had scant experience of the former and no wish to try the latter—and woe betide the woman who attempted to change his mind.

Raking his hands back through his hair, he felt the welcome subsidence of desire. The memory of her would soon be forgotten. He would have his assistant bring him coffee and he would listen to what this unannounced woman wished to say to him.

And then he would go home and take a long, hot shower before going out for dinner. Xavier gave a brief, hard smile at his reflection in the mirror.

Wasn't freedom the most delicious thing?

Perched on the edge of a scarlet sofa which clashed with the expensive suit she was wearing, which she still wasn't quite used to, Laura glanced around.

Over the past few weeks she had had a crash-course in expensive luxury, which had culminated in a stay in an ancient palace in a wildly dramatic country. She had thought that such opulence couldn't be topped—but the offices of Xavier de Maistre came pretty close.

The huge room resembled a luxurious home, rather than the nerve-centre of the successful corporation it undoubtedly was—with cream walls and sumptuous fittings. The chandelier which glistened and danced from the high ceiling looked priceless, and the rather old-fashioned oil paintings of horses and riverbanks gave the place a very traditional and masculine feel.

Carefully, Laura smoothed her fingertips down over her new silk skirt, still getting used to the feel of it. Touching the sensuous material made her shiver—but then these expensive new fabrics felt so different against her skin.

She was scared—or maybe nervous would be a better way to describe it—but she was confident that she was well prepared. Preparation was the number one lesson of being a good lawyer, and although she might not be a great success in other areas of her life Laura had worked very hard to become a good lawyer.

Her mind skated over what she already knew about Xavier de Maistre—international businessman and playboy, and France's reluctant sex-symbol.

A powerful man, with a powerful reputation. He held a vast property portfolio in Paris—as well as in London and New York—and recently the papers had been speculating that he was soon to start a low-cost airline, operating out of Orly airport.

Which meant, of course, that he might not be impressed by what she was about to tell him—and the money which might soon be his. Money—certainly in Laura's experience—only really mattered if you didn't have very much of it.

She heard the lift doors slide open and sat up expectantly, but it was not Xavier de Maistre who emerged but a beautiful blonde woman, who gave Laura a look which was halfway between sympathy and envy.

'Take a tip from me, honey,' she drawled. 'He's great in the sack—but men like de Maistre are *bad news*!'

'I'll bear that in mind,' said Laura politely, though her heart had started hammering, adding to her already nervous state.

Xavier's cool-looking assistant had scrambled to her feet—as if she was about to rugby-tackle the blonde—but the woman was already flying out of the revolving glass doors, so the assistant gave Laura a *can-you-believe-it?* shrug and sat down again.

Laura blinked—because to be honest she didn't usually inhabit the kind of world where women flounced out of sleek offices, giving opinions on the sexual prowess of the man in charge of them!

'Is this an inconvenient time?' she questioned awkwardly.

'But surely you do not care whether it is inconvenient or not?' challenged a soft, silken voice from behind her. 'Since you walk in off the street, demanding to see me—as though I am as accessible to you as turning on a tap.'

Laura rose to her feet and turned around, her mouth

opening to voice her rehearsed little apology—but the words froze on her lips. Of course legendary playboys were always going to be mouthwateringly good-looking, and his reputation had already preceded him—but the reality of seeing Xavier de Maistre in the flesh for the very first time hit her hard. Harder than she had expected. Laura blinked at him foolishly, like a woman who had never seen a man before. But in truth didn't it feel a little like that, because she had never seen anyone quite like *him*?

Legs slightly parted, hands splayed rather arrogantly on narrow hips, he stood like a man with all the confidence in the world—his whole stance one of sexual appeal and authority.

She had seen photographs of Xavier de Maistre—a whole glossy black-and-white set of them—and remembered dispassionately noting a curved beak of a nose and a mouth which was both sensual and cruel. She had known that his skin was darker than most of his race, and now she knew why. But what she had not been expecting was that his physical presence should be so...so...

A peculiar feeling washed over her.

So *overwhelming*.

His deep olive colouring contrasted against the pale and exquisitely cut suit he wore, which was set off by a silk shirt and silk tie. Yet, although he carried the outfit off with the kind of sensual panache the world automatically expected of a Frenchman, his hard and lean body seemed almost too *rugged* to be constrained by the expensive clothes. As if he should be wearing something much rougher, and more basic, or...or...

Or he should be wearing nothing at all!

Now, what on earth had made her think *that*? Laura didn't do the sudden lust thing—and hadn't that been thrown in her face as both her strength and her weakness? Her eyes widened. She was shocked at the progression of her thoughts, but unable to tear her eyes away from him.

He seemed to dominate the room with his compelling charisma, but it was his eyes which drew her in the most—brilliant black eyes that had her fixed firmly in their sight, the coldest and cruellest eyes she had ever seen.

'You do not answer me,' he observed. 'I should have thought that someone who had the temerity to walk in off the streets expecting to see Xavier de Maistre would have had a million smooth remarks to make.' *But your eyes are too busy devouring me,* he thought, without surprise.

With an effort, Laura dragged her mind back to the real reason she was here. 'I know this is an unconventional approach,' she conceded.

So she was English. 'Such understatement is typical of your country,' he observed smoothly. 'Are you selling something?'

She stared at him, shocked. Did she look like a saleswoman in this outfit, which had cost as much as she normally earned in a month? 'No.'

He was staring at her quizzically, but inside he was racking his brains. Had he met her? *Non.* He would have remembered. His eyes ran over her in swift assessment—yet he was having difficulty categorising her, and he was perplexed as to what made her seem so... He frowned. So *different*.

Was it her hair? A deep, dark mass which was lit with red, making her skin look almost snow-white against its intensity? Or was it her eyes—surely the most beautiful eyes he had ever seen? Large and wide, and as green as the most expensive emeralds which were for sale in the jewellery shops in the Avenue Georges V, just along the road.

Her figure was slim, but unfashionably feminine—with rounded breasts and a tiny waist which made the most of the curve of her hips. Clearly she had dressed to suit her shape, for she was wearing a suit—but a suit made of claret-coloured silk, which took the edge off its functional nature. With it she wore a wicked pair of shoes, made of the softest and sexiest suede he had ever seen. Their high heels accentuated the curve of her narrow ankles, and Xavier suddenly got a vivid and erotic image of what it might be like if those ankles were wrapped around his naked back...

He swallowed, and cursed himself for not having satisfied his sexual hunger earlier, when he had had the chance. But he had always prided himself in being able to quell desire at will, and he did it now.

'Haven't you heard of the telephone?' he questioned sarcastically, in an accent as smooth as honey, underpinned with steel. 'Didn't it occur to you to try the normal channels to set up a meeting with me?'

And risk him questioning her about just *why* she wanted to see him? He might have accused her of being mad—and wasn't there a part of her which wouldn't have blamed him?

'Of course it did,' she answered carefully. 'But I had my reasons for this somewhat unusual approach.'

'Did you? How very intriguing.' His eyes narrowed, for there was something about her attitude towards him that he wasn't used to, and he couldn't quite put his finger on it. Because she was not quite as adoring as women usually were? Or maybe because she was not displaying quite the right amount of deference? 'Who are you?' he questioned softly.

His black gaze seemed to scorch over her skin, and suddenly Laura wasn't sure. The mind which had been trained to sift information and compartmentalise it suddenly became a jumble as her thoughts trickled through it like a sieve.

All she was aware of was the magnetic quality of his stare, and the coiled power of his hard body, and the way that it seemed to make her want to…to…

It made her want to despair—because this was business; strictly business.

Or was it?

Because if she looked beyond the professional to the personal for once she could recognise the impact of what she was about to do. And somehow this didn't *feel* quite like business.

Didn't the information she was going to give to

Xavier de Maistre have the potential to change his life—
or certainly the way he thought about life? Laura knew
that she must play this very carefully—she *must*—
because she was in possession of emotional dynamite,
and she did not want it exploding in her face.

Extending her hand towards him, she gave her most
brisk smile, which she hoped masked her sudden lurch
of misgiving and the effect he was having on her.

'My name is Laura Cottingham,' she said.

'Laura,' he repeated, rolling the 'r' around his
tongue and somehow making her Christian name
sound unbelievably sexy. Black brows arched in
question as he caught her slim fingers within his grasp
to shake her hand, allowing his thumb to slide over her
narrow wrist, where he could feel the rapid beating of
her pulse. She was as slim as a young tree, he
thought—and probably just as supple. 'Do I know you?
Your face is unfamiliar to me, and I never forget a
beautiful face.'

Beautiful—her? Expert cosseting expressly for this
unusual job had brought out the best in her, but Laura
would never have described herself as beautiful. How
could she when all her life she'd been chasing her tail,
trying to make something of herself? Only to fall
straight into an unsuitable relationship with someone
who'd made her feel positively *ugly* inside.

Her throat constricted as she felt the warmth of his
skin, the subtle caress of his fingertips, and she pulled her
hand away. 'No,' she said breathlessly. 'We've never met.'

'So why are you here?' he questioned, as his black gaze seared over her like a spotlight. 'Why do you even now hesitate to tell me your business when most would have babbled it for fear that I would kick them out onto the *boulevard*?' he said softly. 'I am intrigued, Mademoiselle Cottingham, and intrigue is such a tantalisingly rare sensation for a man like me.'

A man like me. He was arrogance personified, and yet he had the looks and the charisma to be able to get away with it. How much would he be forgiven, she wondered, simply because his eyes were like dark fire and his face was that of a fallen angel?

Laura shot a look at his assistant, who was watching and listening to the proceedings with rapt attention— even if she was pretending not to. Concentrate on the job, Laura told herself.

'I'd prefer it if we spoke alone,' she said.

Now, why would that be? Xavier's eyes narrowed. Did she think that her beauty allowed her to simply name her terms? And then he stilled as another, darker possibility dawned on him—one which had been tried and had failed on many occasions.

'You're trying to tell me it's a paternity claim?' he demanded softly, and saw her recoil in something like shock. 'You are here on behalf of a girlfriend?'

'No, no. Nothing like that.' Laura shook her head, but then realised with a sudden sense of confusion that unwittingly Xavier de Maistre had put his finger on *exactly* what it was. Just not in quite the same way as he thought. 'I simply think it's better if we have this conversation in private.'

His eyes fixed on her assessingly, as if he were trying to look deep into her mind and read her thoughts—so that by the time he dragged his gaze away Laura felt as if she had been stripped bare.

'*Eh, bien.* We will go into my office, *cherie*,' he agreed softly. 'But it had better be worth it—for I do not like having my time wasted.'

He turned and began to walk towards a door at the far end of the large room, and—her heart beating with nerves at the thought of what she was to do—Laura picked up her briefcase and followed him into an inner sanctum.

'Shut the door,' he said, turning round to watch her wiggle her way in. Had she deliberately worn a close-fitting skirt and high heels, knowing that they would make her walk in a certain way that all red-blooded men would find irresistible?

Laura pushed the door to and faced him, suddenly feeling daunted by the fact that she really *was* alone with him. He hadn't asked her to sit down, so she stood in the middle of the vast room, holding her briefcase and feeling like a traveller who had just missed her train.

'It's kind of you to see me so promptly, Monsieur de Maistre,' she said softly.

'I can assure you that it was not *kindness* which motivated me—it was convenience. You see, you did me a kind of favour, Mademoiselle Cottingham. You provided me with an escape route from a situation which had become rather…tedious.' Black brows were raised imperiously as he waited for her to pry, as women inevitably did—particularly when they were scoring points off one another. But, to his surprise, she did not pursue it. Just gave him a cool, almost glacial smile, which was not the way that women usually looked at him at all.

Laura knew that it was not her place to comment on his arrogance—or to pull him up on his cruel hint about getting rid of the blonde. Yet she suddenly felt an overwhelming pang of sympathy for the woman who had flounced out of the office. He was an easy man to desire, she suspected—and a hard man to leave if he rejected you.

'I would have made another appointment if today had been inconvenient,' she said quietly, as she began to open her case. 'But my brief was to make sure that I spoke with you face to face.'

Something in her tone and her words aroused Xavier's survival instincts, and he suddenly realised his first impression had been right—there was something in her demeanour which did not add up.

People usually came to him because they wanted something. When a man was as powerful and as wealthy as he was, there were few things in life which came without a price.

Laura Cottingham's manner was pleasant, but brisk, efficient and matter-of-fact—the manner of someone who was doing the giving, not taking, and suddenly he was intrigued. *My brief,* she had said.

'Your brief?' he shot out.

'Yes.'

'You are a lawyer?'

'Yes.'

He paused very deliberately. 'I don't trust lawyers unless they're working for me,' he said softly.

'That's probably a very healthy instinct.'

She obviously expected him to laugh, but he did not. His laughter was rare, and usually controlled—for laughter made you vulnerable and he was never that. 'Why did you not contact my own lawyers if it is a legal matter?' he questioned silkily.

'Because…' Laura hesitated. 'Because this a delicate matter for nobody's ears other than your own.'

Her words were tantalising—deliberately so, he suspected.

'How intriguing,' he murmured. 'Tell me, do you like to tease and play games? Are you like this in bed? Or are you going to stop being coy and tell me more?'

Laura flushed deeply at his sexual taunt, but she was in no position to flounce out—and the best way to deal with such behaviour was to ignore it.

'Certainly, Monsieur de Maistre,' she said crisply. 'I'm actually here on behalf of someone else. As a representative of Sheikh Zahir of Kharastan.'

Xavier stilled. He was rarely surprised by anything, but this woman had succeeded in doing just that, and—

inexplicably—his heart missed a beat. A sheikh? Yet he had no business interests in that part of the world. 'I do not understand,' he said softly.

'I don't expect you to. But I will attempt to explain.' Laura took a deep breath, remembering her plan for how best to broach this. 'You have heard of Kharastan, perhaps?'

'I have heard of most countries.' He stared at her unhelpfully.

'You know that it's an extremely wealthy mountain state, which borders on the ancient country of Maraban?'

She was met with an obdurate expression of pure steel.

'I do not need a geography lesson from you,' he said, in a voice which was soft with menace. 'And neither do I need you preparing the ground to cushion the effect of what it is you are about to say. You have been granted access to me and my time is precious! So, either you tell me why you are here, or you get out.'

Laura had been intending to lead into the subject gradually—but she could see the impatience sizzling from him, the irritation which was burning from his black eyes, and she knew that there was no time for any groundwork.

'I'm here to talk about your father,' she said quietly.

Xavier froze as if she had turned him to stone, but beneath the stone his heart gave a strange and painful lurch as she strayed into forbidden territory. He took a step closer to her, lowering his voice so that it was an accusatory whisper.

'How dare you bring up a matter as personal as my parentage?' he questioned menacingly. 'You, who are nothing more than a stranger to me. How *dare* you?'

Laura didn't flinch beneath the accusation which burned from his eyes, telling herself that he had the right to be angry, that anyone would have been angry in similar circumstances.

'I am merely carrying out orders,' she answered, and prayed that she wouldn't stumble over these precious and important words. She was aware of the burden of responsibility which lay so heavily on her shoulders, and suddenly realised that her boss had been economical with the truth. There was no such thing as 'easy money'.

He took a step towards her—the silent menacing step of a predator. 'Whose orders? *Dites-moi,*' he hissed. 'Tell me what you know.'

Laura drew a deep breath, realising that there was no way to prepare for this, or cushion against its impact. He needed to hear the facts in all their stark and compelling simplicity.

'I'm here on a mission because of who you are—or who we think you are. You see, there is reason to believe that you are the son of the Sheikh of Kharastan,' she said quietly.

CHAPTER TWO

XAVIER felt a strange sensation as Laura spoke to him. He could hear a muffled roaring in his ears, and yet he felt curiously detached from his own body. It was as if he had floated up to the summit of the room and was looking down on the scene, in the way people sometimes described a near-death experience.

He was a man who had—necessarily and ruthlessly—subdued anything which came close to emotion. Had that not been the way he had been taught to survive? Yet now he was experiencing feelings which were unsettling him and threatening his equilibrium—and her words seem to echo round and round in his head.

'There is reason to believe you are the son of the Sheikh...'

All he could see was the woman who had come out with such a shocking announcement, with her pale face and her thick dark red hair.

'You lie!' he breathed.

'No! Why would I lie about something like that?'

Logic and reason told him that her statement was nothing but far-fetched fantasy, and yet in the back of Xavier's mind was a nagging doubt which stubbornly refused to be silenced.

For hadn't he always felt that he was different?

He had grown up in poverty in the Marais, in a time before it had become one of the most fashionable places in Paris. During Xavier's youth there had simply been lots of old and dirty houses where artisans would live and work—surrounded by small restaurants, narrow streets and few shops. He and his mother had lived in a tiny garret originally meant for servants—but amid the squalour his mother had worked every hour to provide a good home for her only child.

The exterior of the house in which they'd lived might have been crumbling and depressing, but inside it had been a haven. The walls clean and bright, the curtains crisp and perfectly pressed. There had always been soup or a *pot au feu* bubbling away on the stove—a jug of fresh flowers on the table.

And if his mother had been bitter—so what?—it had been easy to escape from the occasional tense atmosphere at home. If you walked south a block or two you would get to l'Île de la Cité, with the dizzy, imposing height of Notre Dame and the lavish, stained glass splendour of La Sainte-Chapelle.

Sometimes Xavier would go there after school and look at the soaring monuments, and vow that one day he would break free from his poverty stricken world and live surrounded by beauty and space.

His mother had forced books upon her clever son—'For only in education lies an escape from poverty', she'd used to tell him—and she had discouraged him from loitering around the streets with other boys his age.

But Xavier had not cared for the company of his peers, and they had always viewed him with a certain degree of suspicion—his lofty, ambitious attitude and his outstanding looks marking him out. The mane of raven hair, the dark, luminous skin and jewel-black eyes had branded him as someone different from the rest of them.

'Qui est ton père?' the other kids had used to mock him—but Xavier had never answered, for he had not known his father's identity.

Ground vividly into his childhood memory was his mother's tight-lipped fear whenever he had ventured to ask a question about him. Her reluctance to talk.

'He is a powerful and dangerous man who will try to take you away from me. Forget him, Xavier!' was all she would say.

Xavier had been afraid of no one—yet what choice had he had other than to accede to her wishes?

How could he have gone against the woman who had given him life, who had given up all her own ambitions in order to fend for him? Perhaps a part of him had thought she might mellow with age, but his mother had died five years ago—leaving behind nothing but a faded piece of pink ribbon and a gold and ruby ring—and in a way Xavier had felt that he was honouring her memory by letting her secrets die with her.

After that, he had convinced himself that some things were better left alone—that it freed him from burden and complications not to have known the man who was his biological father.

And now this English woman had come here today and was claiming that she knew his identity!

Suddenly Xavier felt anger rising in him, and without warning he reached out and caught hold of her, his fingers gripping into the soft silk which covered her arms. He hauled her up close—close enough to smell the faint scent of lilac she wore, and to see the pulse which beat convulsively against the paper-thin skin at her temple.

'How can my father be a sheikh when I am a Frenchman to every fibre of my being?' he hissed. 'What fairytales do you concoct?'

Laura froze in his grip as his dark features swam in front of her, his breath hot on her face. His eyes were flashing black fire, and she could detect the raw scent of animal passion which clung to his skin. She felt dizzy with his proximity and shook her head, which felt heavy as lead—as if her slender neck did not have the strength to bear the weight of it.

'It isn't a fairytale,' she breathed. 'I swear it isn't!'

'Your word means nothing to me—why should I believe you?' Yet the cold and logical side of his character was already assessing the possibility of the redhead's bizarre declaration being true. *No.* He brought her even closer. 'Who sent you?' he demanded.

His dark-skinned face was so close that her senses were swimming, and Laura could barely get the words out. 'I am acting on the Sheikh's wishes—though he made them known through another.'

'Through another?' he repeated, as if she were speaking in a language he could not understand.

Laura nodded, wishing that her usual crystal-sharp thought processes hadn't deserted her—but how could she concentrate when this man's powerful masculinity seemed to be seeping into her very pores?

'Yes. The Sheikh is old and frail, and thus I dealt mainly through one of his aides.' Laura hesitated. 'His ill-health is one of the reasons he wished to make contact.'

Xavier scowled. The Sheikh's constitution was of no interest to him, but he could not stop the unfamiliar word she had used from stabbing at his heart. *Father.* It was as likely as looking up into the night sky and discovering that the moon had been made of blue cheese all along. As his take on reality shifted and changed irrevocably, he tightened his grip. 'Liar! This man is not my father—how can he be?'

She felt his fingers biting into her flesh. 'It's true, I tell you—it's true. Please. Let me go.'

'Not yet.' He loosened his grip slightly, but he did not set her free. He could see the tremble of her lips and the rush of emotions which her outrageous claim had released were such that he was tempted to drown them all in the sweet oblivion of a punishing kiss.

He could feel the hard, angry nudge of an erection, and for one brief second he wondered how long it would take him to enter her. How quickly could he make her wet with desire and rock against her, relieving these sharp, painful questions with the sweet oblivion of sex?

But as the primitive and powerful animal reaction overwhelmed him, he used his steely will to banish the desire. For now. Because sex would weaken him, would briefly have him in her thrall—and he would not risk that happening until he was acquainted with all the facts.

'Tell me what you know,' he grated.

Laura knew that she had to assert herself before this went any further. That his proximity was too distracting to allow herself any more of it—and it was with a shock like a slap to the face that she recognised that the danger she felt was in part sexual. That she was guilty of desire in a professional setting—and that she was jeapordising all that she had worked for. Oh, Laura—*stop* it, she told herself.

She lifted her chin and her green eyes burned into him. 'Only if you take your hands off me.'

He stared at her for a long, considering moment, his angry black gaze clashing with the emerald fire of hers. 'As you wish,' he ground out.

He dropped his hands so suddenly that Laura was almost caught of balance. Her breath, she realized, was coming in short and unsteady gasps, as if she had come to the end of some long race—but the race, she knew, was only just beginning.

'Now begin!' he ordered, but already rogue thoughts had begun to swim into his mind. Would this woman's statement make some sense of the many questions which had dogged his early years? And yet, in a way, wasn't it almost better if those questions remained unasked?

At the moment Xavier's life was perfectly ordered and exactly as he liked it. He called the shots and had all the control—but now this Englishwoman threatened to lay before him a nest of vipers which one by one would reveal their slithering bodies...

Laura bit her lip. 'Your father is—'

'No!' His voice rang out like a lash of steel. 'You will refer to no one as *my father*. Not when you are recounting this story to me. I do not have a father and I never have had! Do you understand?'

Laura nodded, because this was something she was well-equipped to deal with. Denial. People did it all the time—they buried their heads in the sand and pretended that something wasn't happening because the thought that it was hurt too much.

Hadn't she done it herself with her cheating ex-boy-friend, when the writing had been all over the wall in letters twenty feet high that he no longer wanted her? That he had got what he wanted and after that she was expendable. And hadn't she—like a fool—made excuses for the fact that he had been slowly edging her out of his life and making her into a laughing stock into the bargain? Oh, yes, Laura knew all about denial.

'Very well,' she said calmly. 'How would you like me to tell the story?'

For a moment his black eyes narrowed with suspicion. Was she mocking him? But as he searched her pale face Xavier detected a glimpse of empathy in the shimmering depths of her green eyes and he tensed, for he was not a subject in need of pity.

'You will simply answer my questions. For now.' Drawing his broad shoulders back, he shot her an imperious look. 'Who are you working for?'

Laura nodded. What had Malik said to her? *'Bring the Frenchman back to Kharastan with you, no matter what it takes.'*

'I work for Sheikh Zahir of Kharastan.'

His mouth hardened into a slash of censure, his fists clenching by the shafts of his powerful thighs—and suddenly it became easier to channel his frustration and rage outwards, rather than turn it in on himself.

'And just how do *you* come to be in a position to know all this?' Xavier demanded. 'Are you a hanger-on to this family of sheikhs? One of those women who are turned on by the strong, dark, silent type—perhaps secretly hoping that one of them will whisk you away to his desert tent and ravish you? Is that what turns you on, *cherie*?'

It was clearly intended to be insulting, and it worked—but unfortunately she found his words erotic as well as a slur.

Had she thought this would be easy?

Yes, she had.

Armed with the knowledge that she was about to en-
lighten Xavier de Maistre and tell him that he was the son
of a man so fabulously wealthy that it made your average
billionaire look like a pauper, she had imagined that he
would want to be on the first plane to Kharastan to rove
his eyes greedily over his prospective inheritance.

How wrong could she have been?

He had failed to grab at the carrot she had dangled
before him. Maybe a man as successful as Xavier could
not be bought or even tempted by the lure of a possible
inheritance.

'You say nothing,' he taunted softly. 'And you have
told me nothing of your own place in this unusual desert
hierarchy.'

'I have no place in it,' she answered. 'I'm working
for the royal family of Kharastan; it's as simple as that.
I'm a temporary employee with no agenda of my own.'

'No?' His eyes seared into her. 'Everyone has an
agenda, *cherie.*' Especially when a man was as rich and
as powerful as Xavier was. He had never met anyone
who didn't want *something* from him. 'Tell me, are you
being employed for your legal capabilities—or because
you have beautiful breasts and come-to-bed eyes?'

Laura stared at him. He was making her sound like
some sort of *hooker.* 'I don't have to stand here and be
insulted like that!' she said, in a low, shaking voice.

'You think that it is an insult to be admired for your

very obvious attributes?' he mocked. 'But you are right—you do not have to stay and submit yourself to anything which offends you.' He flared his nostrils like an aristocratic racehorse as he gazed at her with haughty contempt. 'You do not like what I say to you? Then leave—and leave now—for I am not stopping you!'

He was calling her bluff—he knew it and she knew it. But she did not dare leave for fear that she might not get another chance to return and state her case.

What Xavier de Maistre thought of her and said to her was irrelevant—she was here to do a job, that was all, and this was strictly business, not personal.

So *stick* to business, Laura told herself. If he only came up to her knee and had spots all over his face would she be melting in some kind of pathetic pool on the Persian carpet? Of course she wouldn't.

She forced a glossy smile. 'Do you have a photograph of your father here in the office?'

'What do you think?' His gaze flicked over her, icy-black and unfriendly. 'Do *you* keep photos of your parents in your office?'

'I'll take that as a no,' she said quietly, ignoring the sarcasm. 'Would you like to see a photo that I've been given?'

What he would like would be to walk away from the potential dynamite of this situation, but it was already too late. Like being witness to a crime. You couldn't rewind the clock and wish you hadn't seen it because of the complications which would follow in its wake.

'I suspect that you are about to produce one from your bag,' he observed caustically. 'Like a magician performing a trick at a children's party.'

Her fingers were trembling as she unclipped her briefcase and withdrew the card-backed envelope which contained the portrait. She held it out towards him.

Xavier took it from her without a word and sucked in a long, low breath as he stared hard at the photograph.

It was a professional studio portrait, and the man in it had been captured in his most virile prime. Glimpsed beneath a white flowing headdress, held in place with a circlet of knotted gold, his hair was as raven-dark as Xavier's, and the cruel beak of a nose and sensual lips were instantly recognisable.

Xavier felt his throat tighten, for the resemblance was undeniable. 'Okay, so he looks a little like me,' he grated.

A *little*? But Laura said nothing.

'We both have black eyes and hair,' he said with a shrug, and then, when still she said nothing, he lifted his head to stare at her. Without a word, he put the photo down on his desk, then strode over to where Laura had since sat down.

Something in his expression both alarmed and excited her, and she sprang up to face him, trying not to flinch beneath the fierce onslaught of conflicting expressions which had suddenly turned his rugged face into the face of an adversary.

'Where did you get this?' he demanded.

'I told you,' said Laura, her tongue flicking out to

moisten her parched lips as she saw something in his eyes far more threatening than anger or contempt. Something which looked uncomfortably like desire. 'From the man….' She picked the phrase with care, remembering his admonition. 'The man who claims to be your father.'

He made a low, growling sound at the back of his throat, and then, reaching out, he caught hold of her and brought her right up against his hot, hard body—registering with satisfaction but no surprise that her pupils dilated in automatic response and that the tips of her breasts were pushing against the sensually soft material of her suit.

'What do you want from me?' he demanded, but his hand had snaked around her waist and had begun to caress its narrow indentation.

Breathlessly, Laura stared up at him as he began to stroke her, feeling tension coiling at the pit of her stomach, the hot prickling of her breasts, and a kind of dazed incredulity at the situation in which she found herself. This was outrageous! Yet his proximity was nothing short of destabilising—his touch as irresistible as freedom to the caged animal. And, just like an animal, she gave a tiny whimper of disbelief.

Her throat felt so tight that she could barely get the words out. Because this was desire given a whole new meaning. 'I can't think straight when you're…'

'When I am stroking you?' he purred, and he bent his head down to whisper into her ear. She could feel the warm caress of his breath, and his words were the most irresistible sounds she had ever heard. 'But you like me stroking you. You would like me to be stroking you far more intimately, I think….'

With my fingers parting your thighs and touching you where you are like a molten blazing furnace. Touching you until you shudder beneath me and cry out my name, then kissing the sound into silence.

'Stop it,' she said breathlessly, because she could sense his desire—taste and smell it, almost hear it—as if it were thrumming in the air around them. She felt like a piece of wax left in front of the fire, dissolving beneath the warmth of his touch. 'Stop it right now.'

He dropped his hands like a man who had been playing a game he had become bored with, enjoying the sight of her darkened eyes, the way she was trying to gulp air into her lungs and the faint flush which had shaded her pale skin. He would have her—of course he would—*mais pas encore.*

Not yet.

'You still haven't told me what it is you want,' he said tonelessly.

Laura gave herself time to compose herself—to rid herself of the erotic pictures which were playing in slow motion in her protesting brain, and the sensations which were dancing dangerously over her sensitised skin. 'I have orders to bring you back to Kharastan,' she said slowly.

He flexed his long olive fingers and then curled them down into the palms of his hands, so that they resembled the claws of some predatory bird, fixing her in the ebony sight of his gaze as if she were some helpless prey.

'Orders?'

'I'm sorry—that was an inadvisable choice of word.'

'Damned right it was!' he gritted out. 'But the word is not nearly as inadvisable as the sentiment.'

He leaned forward, his eyes spitting fire, so that Laura got some idea of what the coals of hell might look like.

'Do you really think that a man like Xavier de Maistre can be *summoned*?' he demanded. 'Taken to some God-forsaken country to meet a man whom I do not even believe *is* my father?'

Freed from the seduction of his touch, Laura felt reason begin to return—but she knew she could not allow herself the luxury of answering him back. Just stay with it for a little while longer, she urged herself. All she had to do was get him on that plane, and then she would have earned her bonus and need never set eyes on his dangerous, sexy face again.

Once again, Malik's words came back to her.

'Bring the Frenchman back to Kharastan with you, no matter what it takes.'

What would it take? Laura looked around at the costly furnishings. Not a bribe, that was for sure. Nor vague promises that might never been fulfilled.

What would a powerful man like this treasure above all else?

The truth, perhaps?

For what else did she have to offer him?

'I think you may regret it if you do not agree to accompany me,' she said boldly.

Her words did not seem to be what he was expecting. *'Regret?'* he echoed incredulously. 'I can assure
you, *cherie*, that regret is not a part of my nature.'

No, she could imagine that with those cold eyes he
would move restlessly ever forward, like a shark—never
looking back or experiencing that wistful ache that
maybe something should have been done differently.

'I think this may be the exception which proves the
rule,' she said, and sighed, her green eyes troubled as she
looked at him. Because this had now become much
more than a job to be successfully completed. She didn't
really know Xavier—and what she did know of him
she didn't particularly like. Yet deep down he was a
man who risked throwing away an opportunity which
might never come again—and so she spoke to him from
the heart.

'The Sheikh is old and frail,' Laura said softly. 'You
might be right—this whole incident might be the result
of a series of misunderstandings. Perhaps you aren't his
son. But unless you go, you'll never find out. Once you
have the truth, you can reject it if you please—but how
would you feel if he *was* your father and you missed this
opportunity? If you want a chance to meet your father,
then I advise you to act now, before it is too late.' Laura
lifted her chin and met his gaze. 'Because old men can
die at any time, Xavier.'

CHAPTER THREE

THE atmosphere in the sumptuous room changed, became electric—as if the mention of death had somehow charged it with life.

Xavier stared at the woman with the dark red hair and felt the slow, powerful beat of his heart—followed by an odd, inexplicable twist of pain which he quashed as ruthlessly as he would a fly.

Drawing himself up to his full impressive height, Xavier subjected Laura to a stare of insolent question. 'Is there anything else you want to tell me, *cherie*?' he drawled, his rich accent edged with sarcasm. 'Mmm?'

Laura shook her head uncertainly. Hadn't she already said enough?

'No? Not about to disclose that you are working for some cable TV reality show and are carrying a secret camera to film me in the sanctity of my office?'

Laura was about to ask him why he was being so suspicious—until she remember the snatched photos in

Bonjour! magazine. No wonder the black eyes were glittering with such hostility.

'Get out,' he said quietly.

This wasn't how the meeting was supposed to end, and Laura stared at him in disbelief. 'But surely you want to—'

'Do not try to second-guess me!' he interrupted furiously. 'Just go—and go *now*! *Maintenant!*'

Laura looked into his face and read something implacable there, and she knew that further words would be wasted. She nodded and picked up her bag, taking from it one of her business cards which she laid down on the desk. 'That's my mobile number,' she said. 'I'm staying at the Paradis if you want to contact me.'

She went to pick up the photo, but his voice rang out across the office.

'Leave it here,' he ordered. 'If it is—as you say— a photo of my father, then I can lay a greater claim to it than you.'

'But—'

'I said leave it!' he said icily. 'And go.'

Aware of his dark eyes burning into her, Laura made her way across the vast room and somehow managed to walk out of the door with her head held high—but by the time she had re-emerged on the pavement in the fashionable eighth arrondisement her hands were trembling.

Her hotel wasn't that far away—but her fancy new suede shoes were most definitely *not* designed for walking. So she hailed a cab, which crawled through the affluent streets before dropping her at the Paradis.

Was it possible that she had failed in her mission at the first hurdle?

The lift zoomed her up to the vast suite which the Sheikh's aide had insisted on providing for her. Just as he had insisted on supplying a stylist, who had taken her on a comprehensive shopping tour once she had arrived in the city. Because it seemed that although Laura had the brains, the discretion and the qualifications needed for this very unusual job, she did not have the wardrobe to carry her comfortably into the highest echelons of society.

And, whilst her well-pressed navy blue suit and cream blouses were ideal for life as a small-town lawyer, she was infinitely grateful for the couture clothes she was wearing today. Clothes could protect you, she realised. They could make you look the part you were playing—even if inside you felt as insecure as a little child left alone at a party where she didn't know anyone.

Once safely inside the suite, she kicked off her shoes and lay back on the sumptuous hotel bed, staring at the ceiling, wondering what on earth she should do next. Hang around like a puppy dog, waiting to see if Xavier would take the bait and call?

And if he didn't, then what?

Then she would have wasted a perfect opportunity to explore a city she'd never visited before. Time would hang heavily if she just waited, and she would find out soon enough whether or not she would be banking the huge sum of money she had been promised *if* she succeeded in her mission to return with Xavier.

Carefully, Laura took off the new suit and hung it in the wardrobe, enjoying the luxury of choice before pulling on a russet-coloured cashmere dress which should have clashed with her hair but somehow didn't. A gold chain belt and flat brown boots completed the look, and she set off to sightsee. Yes, it would be easy to get used to being a wealthy woman, she decided ruefully.

'Are there any messages for me?' she asked the chic young woman at the reception desk.

'*Non, madesmoiselle,*' the girl replied, with an apologetic shrug.

The major attractions were all within walking distance, but Laura felt as if she was only half there. To the outside world she was aware that she must look like a woman awestruck by the sights of the city, bewitched by the majestic Eiffel Tower which straddled the Trocadero like a giant steel croquet hoop, enchanted with the Sainte-Chapelle, whose glowing stained-glass interior was like being inside a jewelled casket.

But beneath Laura's pleasure ticked the worries which had arisen as the result of her meeting with Xavier, and *her* automatic questions about whether she could have handled it any better.

It had all seemed so simple when her boss had called her into his office to ask whether she would like to take a short sabbatical and earn enough money to substantially reduce her debts by working for the royal house of Kharastan.

Laura had still been reeling from the huge hole in her finances—if not quite her heart—left by her boyfriend Josh's departure, and she had blinked at her boss, wondering if she'd misheard him.

'Working for a royal family?' she had verified.

'That's right.'

'You mean I'd have to fly out to Kharastan?' she asked.

'I certainly do,' replied her boss, smiling. 'All expenses paid. Private jets. Designer clothes—the lot!'

'Don't! It sounds too good to be true,' Laura protested.

'Well, it's not. It's legit.' Her boss smiled. 'I've been approached by a friend of a friend—that's how these things work. They want a lawyer who's young, enthusiastic, discreet and…female.'

'Why female?' she asked.

Her boss gave her a wry look. 'Women bring a different dimension to matters which have the potential to be emotionally explosive—which this one does.'

'But it's…safe?'

He burst out laughing. 'Hell, yes! You're a single woman, and you'd be under the protection of the Sheikh himself in a notoriously strict and old-fashioned country—you'll be as safe as houses!'

It had sounded so easy. Too easy, she now realised— or perhaps she hadn't actually taken into account how the illegitimate son would react to such a piece of news.

Yet maybe she should have done. She should have

had the sense to realise that reactions to events weren't straightforward. You could never predict the outcome to a situation, because people weren't predictable.

Laura walked slowly back to the Paradis, wondering just what to do next. Should she ring the Sheikh and tell him about Xavier's initial reaction? Or give the Frenchman time to mull it over?

She was so deep in thought as she walked into the foyer that she barely registered the man who sat in the shadows, observing her with eyes that gleamed like jet.

Who then rose noiselessly to his feet to follow her, his grim gaze never leaving the provocative sway of her bottom.

Laura had just walked into her suite, and was preparing to close the door when it was levered open. Her automatic open-mouthed fear was not banished when she saw that it was Xavier.

'What the hell are you doing?' she cried, as he shut the door behind him as if he had some inalienable right to do so.

'What does it look like ? You wanted to talk, didn't you?' His voice dipped into a caress of pure silk. 'Well, here I am, *cherie*…all yours.'

Had he intended to make that remark sound tinged with sexual promise? And did he know that it had worked? 'I would have liked a little notice,' she said breathlessly, her fingers flying to her bare throat. 'Being jumped on like that isn't my idea of fun.'

A nerve flickered at his cheek and an added tension

crept into his body. 'No? Then you have not lived. And anyway—I thought you liked the element of surprise,' he drawled softly, enjoying the soft creep of colour into her cheeks which followed his sexual taunt. 'Wasn't that precisely how you ambushed me?'

Laura attempted a smile, but it wasn't easy—not when he was looking at her that way. Did he look at all women as if he could melt their clothes off their body with that sizzling black stare? And did some treacherous side of them always want him to? Assert yourself. Sound professional. Pretend he's just walked into your office. 'Would you like to sit down?'

He glanced around the room, his gaze coming to rest on the vast four-poster bed. 'And where should we sit…over there? Wouldn't that provide something of a distraction? I don't know about you—but I would find it very difficult not to get horizontal if I was on a bed with a woman as beautiful as you.'

Laura's heart hammered. 'Don't be disgusting.'

'Disgusting? All I'm doing is telling the truth. I wonder, are you always so uptight, *cherie*?' Her body belied her words, he noted with satisfaction, as he saw the tips of her breasts harden in response to his words, outlined with disturbing detail through the fine material of her dress.

Ruthlessly he dragged his thoughts away from the physical—there would be time enough for that. 'But let us forget about the bed and all its delightful possibilities and concentrate on the matter in hand.' His eyes glittered. 'I want some answers.'

Laura nodded. Answers she could deal with. 'That's what I'm here for. Ask away,' she said.

'You think that—even if I had the desire—I could just drop everything and travel east with you?'

'Of course. You're the boss—a powerful man who can do as he pleases.'

'You flatter me.'

'I wasn't intending to.'

'Weren't you? Don't you know that all men love to be flattered?'

'It isn't something I've made a special study of,' she said archly, something in his taunting tone making her forget her vow to keep this on a strictly business level. 'And perhaps some men have had a little too much of it all their lives. I suspect you might be in that category, Monsieur de Maistre.'

Xavier gave the kind of smile a wolf might give to a helpless lamb before he devoured it. With her defiance, she had sealed her fate—for no conquest was more exciting than that of a woman who was trying very hard not to be interested.

Why had she been chosen for this job? he wondered. Was she bait, designed to bring him back to the Sheikh—chosen for her particular type of beauty to ensnare him as women had ensnared men since the beginning of time?

Should he test her out? Kiss her now? Quell his anger and frustration at her revelation by losing himself in the softness of her lips? But lovemaking would distract him from this curious dilemma he found himself in.

Ever since he had ordered her out of his office his thoughts had been in turmoil, and it was not a state he usually experienced. He despised being at the mercy of such feelings—but it was as if a silent and very necessary battle was taking place inside him.

The cold, calculating side of his character was telling him that there was no point discovering a father at this stage in his life—even if her bizarre claim *should* turn out to be true, which he doubted. He didn't need a father.

He had made a success of his life and he had done it on his own terms—it was not in his character to yearn for some kind of reunion. More importantly, he foresaw a million complications—both practical and emotional—should he choose to pursue this line of action.

Yet her astounding revelation had awoken a curiosity inside him, and he knew that to leave the possibility unexplored would be to leave him with a lasting sense of regret. And—as he had already said—he didn't *do* regret.

And wasn't there an added enticement which would make the trip worthwhile? The thought of bedding the delectable Laura Cottingham, who was doing her best to pretend she wasn't interested! Xavier gave a slow, steady smile of anticipation.

'You are right,' he said slowly. 'I can do as I please—within reason. I have never in my life received such an intriguing invitation issued by such an irresistible woman—how could any man refuse it? So you can lose the look of anxiety which is tightening those pretty lips and relax, *cherie*—for I will return to Kharastan with you.'

For a moment Laura could hardly believe what she was hearing—she had been so convinced that he would do the opposite.

'I'm very…pleased,' she said, aware that it was a ridiculous word to use—but her relief was tempered by a prickly awareness that she was dealing with a man who spelt danger, and that was sending her thoughts haywire.

'I expect you are,' he said coolly, because he needed to maintain control in this extraordinary situation—and in order to do that he needed to keep her guessing. She must be in *his* power. She would be his to control and his to command. 'But I am not there yet, so I suggest you contain your excitement until then.'

Laura nodded. 'A car will pick you up at nine-thirty tomorrow morning and take you to the airfield, if that suits?'

'It doesn't.'

'It *doesn't*?'

Xavier allowed himself a smile—a devilish curve of his lips which hinted at a wicked kind of pleasure. His peers at La Bourse—Paris's famous stock exchange, built by Napoleon himself—would have trembled if they had seen that smile.

'*Non.* I do not think you understand how I operate, *cherie.* You will not dictate a time nor a place nor a method of travelling,' he demurred silkily. 'You will fit in with *me.*'

'I'm not quite sure I…understand,' said Laura unsteadily.

'It is quite simple. I intend to arrange my own transport to Kharastan.'

Laura stared at him. 'But that's crazy!' she protested. 'The Sheikh has a luxury aircraft ready and waiting to fly you there at a moment's notice.'

'You think I am tempted by a *luxury aircraft*?'

'No, of course not. I didn't—'

'I will not be beholden to the Sheikh,' interjected Xavier. 'These are my terms, and either you accept them or you return empty-handed—for I will not compromise and neither will I change my mind.'

The steely glint of determination in his eyes told Laura that he meant it, and there was a pause as she looked at him speechlessly. Because what *could* she say? He had her over a barrel, and he knew it.

'But there's no direct flight to Kharastan,' she pointed out. 'It could take ages to pick up connections.'

His eyes mocked her. 'You think I fly on scheduled airlines? I will use the charter company that I always use. At least I can entrust them with my life.'

'And what's that supposed to mean?'

'Think about it. If I am, as you say, the son of the Sheikh—then surely it is in the interests of more than one member of his family to wish me harm.'

She wanted to tell him that people didn't think or act like that—until she remembered the dizzying array of events which had led her to this bizarre moment, and suddenly anything seemed possible.

But it was not the imagined threat of physical danger

which had set Laura's senses tingling with fear—but the real and present risk of being in this man's presence. Of this terrible, almost aching awareness of his powerful sensuality.

Xavier's eyes narrowed as they raked over her face. So pure, he thought. So white. So…wary. He felt his loins tighten. 'What is the matter, *cherie*?' he mocked softly. 'You look nervous.'

'Why on earth would I be nervous, Monsieur de Maistre?'

'I think we both know the answer to that.' His eyes flashed. 'And perhaps you had better start calling me Xavier from now on.'

He was only telling her to use his Christian name— yet with that rich, French accent which flowed over her skin like silk it sounded as if he was suggesting a breath-taking intimacy.

Laura looked into the mocking depths of those eyes, and suddenly she was scared.

CHAPTER FOUR

'WE WILL be landing in just under an hour, *monsieur*.'

Xavier glanced up from the sheaf of papers he had been studying and into the doe-like eyes of the beautiful stewardess.

'*Merci bien,*' he said, and turned his gaze to Laura, who was sitting opposite him, reading, in the opulent cabin of the aircraft, which had been created to resemble a rather smart salon.

She had surprised him during the flight for he had expected her to babble, to make conversation just for the sake of it, as women inevitably did—never seeming to realise that silence could sometimes be the most alluring quality of all. But instead she had picked up a rather serious-looking novel and proceeded to read it.

It was ironic that for once he could have used some inane chatter in order to distract him from the troubling nature of his thoughts.

Last night his sleep had been haunted with strange, disturbing dreams, and he had woken with a start. He had sat up in the bed of his Parisian apartment, his body naked amid the rumpled sheets, and stared into the black mantle of the night—aware that the Englishwoman had forced him to address an area of his life which had always been a mystery. Even if her claim were true he was unsure whether he wanted that mystery revealed— and yet somehow he felt compelled to commence this voyage of discovery by something he hadn't known was within him.

For a man used to being in control, it had unsettled him. But Xavier had done what he did best—compartmentalized, shutting out the disquieting feelings and the *what ifs* with a steely determination. What was the point in trying to imagine what he might find when they landed in Kharastan when they would be there soon enough?

So he had brought work with him for the journey and attacked it with his usual thoroughness. But now he had finished he was left alone with thoughts he would have preferred not to have. And the glossy redhead was not paying him the deference he would normally have expected—which of course made him want her all the more. Desire was something he could deal with—far less disturbing than the subject of his identity. Desire had a beginning and a conclusion, and once he had this Laura Cottingham under his spell he would tire of her.

'You would like something more to eat?' he queried softly. 'Or to drink?'

Laura looked up from her book and wondered if he had noticed her reading and re-reading words which had been stubbornly refusing to make any sense. He was a difficult man to concentrate around.

'No, thanks. I'm not hungry.'

'But you barely touched your lunch,' he observed.

This was true. The perfectly poached piece of fish and green vegetables had failed to appeal—and even a chocolate extravagance of a pudding which would have normally had her drooling back home in England on a night out with the girls had made her feel very slightly queasy.

She could blame her lack of appetite on the flight—but that would have been a lie. The plane journey had been smooth and noiseless—with only the slightest turbulence when they were flying over the mountainous terrain of Dashabhi.

No, her lack of appetite and extraordinary feelings of self-consciousness could be attributed to one cause and one cause only—and it was sitting staring at her now.

'Women don't eat as much as men,' she answered stoutly.

The black gaze changed direction, lingering appreciatively on the outline of her legs, which were stretched out in front of her. 'English women never eat properly,' he observed caustically. 'They skip breakfast and eat crisps for lunch.'

'Well, actually I never eat crisps—I wouldn't be able to deal with clients all afternoon if I existed on junk food. And, as well as being an outrageous generalization, I really don't think my dietary habits are a suitable subject for discussion, do you?'

'*Au contraire,*' he demurred, because flirting was a lot easier to deal with than thinking about what might lie ahead. And her lawyer's tongue was sharp enough to make him want to pit his wits against her. 'If you do not want a man to remark on your sensational body, *cherie*, then you should not show it off in quite such a way.'

Laura looked down at herself as if her outfit had been replaced while she had been reading without her noticing—as if she might suddenly find herself sitting there in a skimpy little bikini. But of course her new wardrobe was still taking a bit of getting used to.

The stylist had chosen clothes for Paris and clothes for Kharastan—and the two were vastly different. Paris was cling and Kharastan was camouflage, and today she had dressed accordingly—in a manner befitting an employee of the Sheikh soon to arrive in a land where women's clothes were expected to be modest.

From neck to ankle she was covered in a long-sleeved dress of pure silk in a pale buttermilk colour. A fairly demure split went only as far as the knee—and that was to facilitate movement rather than to show off any leg. Gold sandals shimmered on her bare feet, and the only real extravagance was a pair of heavy and intricate dangling earrings set with beautiful deep green stones.

'But I am not dressed provocatively!' she defended.

'No?' He raised a dark brow. 'Surely that dress was designed to emphasise the very feminine shape beneath? One of those cleverly cut shapes which is supposed to be modest and yet looks anything but—particularly to a member of the opposite sex. Sometimes concealment can be unbearably exciting, as I am sure you know. I commend your taste, *cherie*.'

He was making her sound like some kind of temptress who had deliberately set out to seduce him! Should she tell him that this was a million miles from what she would normally have worn? That she had been guided by the expert eye of a stylist employed to dress her by Sheikh Zahir? But why tell him more than he needed to know? That sort of information would probably result in him interrogating her as to what she usually *did* wear, and then no doubt those intelligent black eyes would narrow and that sexy voice would start asking her even more personal questions.

And she didn't want to get personal with him, for that way lay danger—instinct told her so. In the past, she had been guilty of ignoring her gut feelings—of doing what she believed was the right thing to *do* instead of what she knew in her heart to be right for *her*. But not any more. From now on she stayed true to herself—and a cool, professional distance was exactly what was required.

Laura looked at him. After telephoning the Sheikh's disbelieving and angry aide last evening to tell him that Xavier had stubbornly insisted on arranging his own transport, she had done a lot of thinking.

It seemed to be a given that Xavier was going to flirt outrageously with her. He was good-looking and he was French—and even if he was only half-French weren't they a race of men who prided themselves on being superlative lovers? And if the rest of his blood really *was* that of a royal sheikh—sheikhs also being renowned for their sexual prowess—then *of course* he was going to behave in a way Laura wasn't used to. A totally inappropriate way—or was that just her lack of experience?

There weren't many men who looked like *him* strutting around the small town of Dolchester. If there had been then she might have gained a little practice in dealing with them and been better equipped at coping with Xavier de Maistre.

No, a man of this calibre was outside her experience—and just because she had been employed to accompany him back to Kharastan that did not mean that she had to put up with his blatantly sexual scrutiny or provocative remarks. Hadn't she decided after the Josh debacle that never again would she let a man take advantage of her?

The pilot's voice informed them that they were cruising at a steady altitude and would shortly be beginning their descent. Soon she would step out onto the tarmac at Kumush Ay—the capital city of Kharastan—and her job would be completed. It was no longer essential for her to maintain the effort of trying to placate him—she could stop walking on eggshells.

That did not mean that she was about to start being rude to him, of course—simply that she might open his eyes to the way that most women liked to be treated. It might do him good.

'Monsieur de Maistre,' she sighed.

'I keep telling you to call me Xavier,' he interjected silkily, aware that her reluctance to do so had intrigued him.

'Xavier,' Laura agreed, and then hesitated. How could his name be so…so…*enticing*? Because it was so foreign to her lips—lingering there like the juice of a fruit she had never tasted before? Or because it was impossible to say it without first softening your voice? She swallowed. 'I really don't think it's appropriate for you to make comments about my figure, or my choice of apparel.'

He laughed softly. 'Apparel?' he echoed. Was this the stiff, starchy attitude so beloved of generations of Englishmen—because they wanted their women to sound like their nannies? 'But you are a woman—do you not care to be admired?'

Laura sat up straight and looked at him reprovingly. 'Obviously, if I find myself in a situation where such a reaction might be more relevant.'

'Such as?'

'Well, at a party. Or a social function.' Laura shrugged. 'Something like that.'

'You think that men and women only play with one another when they meet *socially*?' he demanded incredulously.

Play with one another. Unwanted images swam into Laura's mind as she recalled the way her blood had pounded when he had gripped her arms, the melting way he had made her feel inside. Now he was threatening to do the same again if she let him—just by the outrageous taunts he was making and the way he was looking at her.

'Why do you twist my words round?' she demanded. 'Can't you get it into your head that not every woman with a pulse wants to leap into bed with you?'

There was a pause, and when he spoke his eyes were glittering.

'Whoever said anything about leaping into bed, Laura?' he questioned softly, enjoying her answering rise of colour.

'Oh!' Laura glared at him. This was madness. She *had* to get a grip of herself before they landed. Malik had hinted that other work might be available to her once this job was over, but he was hardly going to be impressed if she was in emotional tatters by the time she arrived. 'I think I *would* like that drink, if it's all the same to you,' she said.

'Me, too,' he said, pressing a button by his seat to summon the stewardess. He spoke rapidly in his native tongue and the girl disappeared into the galley.

Laura met his eyes. He was staring at her as if he would like to jump on her and eat her up, and she wished he would do up the top button of his shirt. That crisp, dark hair peeping out was *very* distracting. 'This may be the last proper drink you get for a while,' she said. 'I suppose you're aware that alcohol is frowned on in Kharastan?'

'How kind of you to alert me to local custom,' he

observed sarcastically. 'And there I was thinking that it would be one long booze-fest from dawn to dusk!'

Laura bit back a smile, because surely to admit that she found him amusing would be another admission of weakness—and hadn't she demonstrated enough of that already?

'Your English is pretty amazing,' she observed instead. 'Did you learn it as a little boy?'

The shutters came down. 'But surely you know everything there is to know about my early life?' he questioned softly. 'Hasn't your Sheikh had a report made on me?'

Stupidly, Laura felt herself blushing. 'Well, yes—he did, actually,' she said awkwardly.

'Let me see it.'

For a second Laura hesitated—but only for a second. What was the point in trying to refuse him when his look of unyielding determination told her it would be pointless? Pulling out the report from her briefcase, she handed it to him, meeting the question in his eyes with a shrug.

'I was only doing my job,' she said.

He noted her defensive tone with a grim kind of pleasure. How it would have pleased him to have taken the moral high-ground with her—to scorn her for invading his personal space—and yet hadn't he done similar, or worse? In the past, hadn't he been called unscrupulous in his business dealings—been both lauded and feared for his cold-hearted determination to succeed?

Yet you don't like it when it is done to you, do you?

His eyes scanned the notes, which were gratifyingly

brief—simply stating that his home had been in the Marais. There was his school record, naturally, and a list of his mother's patchy employment history—it had suited her and her employers for her to be paid cash-in-hand, so that her name appeared as infrequently as possible on national records.

He saw now why the newspapers had always come up with a blank whenever they had tried to investigate his past. Apart from a few non-starter articles by a couple of ex-schoolfriends—who had provided the unsurprising facts that as a youth he had been a bit of a loner and popular with the girls—there had been nothing. 'Not very much,' he observed.

'Surprisingly little,' agreed Laura.

So his mother's wish had been granted, he thought, in a rare moment of reflection. She had strived for and achieved a private life which had bordered on the secretive. Had that contributed to his cool detachment—his almost icy indifference to relationships which women had always complained about?

He stared at Laura. 'Does he have sons of his own?' he questioned suddenly. 'I mean legitimate sons?'

'No,' she answered slowly. 'He has no legitimate sons.'

'So maybe he's clutching at straws—desperate to find someone he can call his own. What exactly is the purpose of this trip?' Xavier questioned.

Laura saw the way his mouth hardened. 'Isn't it obvious?'

'Is it? A reunion inspired by sentiment or practicality, I wonder?' he queried, his voice brittle with sarcasm. 'Does a powerful man ache to see his seed made flesh before he passes from this world into the next? Or is he planning to allocate his riches to a man who grew up in relative poverty?' His black eyes glittered. 'Do you think I am about to inherit a vast fortune, *cherie*?'

'That's a very mercenary attitude,' she said.

'You think so?' He shook his dark head. '*Non*. I am merely being practical. Or would you think it more appropriate if I affected wide-eyed surprise if such an offer was made to me?'

'That's what most people would do,' she said, thinking about the readings of wills she'd had to deal with during the course of her career, and the baser instincts it brought out in people.

'Well, I don't need or want his damned money!' continued Xavier, as if she hadn't spoken. 'Even sheikhs must learn that loyalty and affection cannot just be bought at the end of a lifetime.'

It seemed a curiously *moral* attitude for a notorious playboy to have, and was an insight into a character Laura suspected was far more complex than it first seemed.

The stewardess chose that moment to arrive with the wine, and Laura was glad to have the distraction of dark burgundy being poured into crystal glasses. She took a large mouthful.

'Is that better?' he questioned softly.

'Much better. It's delicious.'

Xavier sipped his own wine as he watched her, aware that the balance of information was tipped heavily in her favour. What did he know of her, after all? Wasn't it perhaps time he started to even things up? 'So, tell me about your connection with the royal family of Kharastan.'

It was more a command than a question. 'I have been in the employ of the Ak Atyn family for a month.'

'Only a month?' Xavier's eyes narrowed. 'So short a time to be entrusted with such a *personal* matter.'

'I was employed by Sheikh Zahir specifically for this purpose,' she said softly.

'To bring me to him?'

'That's right. I'm an expert on family law—and all Kharastani legal documents are drawn up in English, too.'

'So how come a nice girl like you ends up running errands for a sheikh?'

'Thank you for your supposition that I'm nice.'

'Don't you have a boyfriend who minds you going on missions to ensnare strange Frenchmen?'

Laura raised her eyebrows. 'Why would he mind? Are you one of those men who thinks a woman needs permission to breathe?'

'So you *do* have a boyfriend?'

'Actually, I don't.' Now, why had she told him *that*? 'And is my personal life really relevant?'

Xavier made a small sound of exasperation. '*Alors!* Why do lawyers never answer questions directly?'

'Perhaps because we are paid to ask them, not to

answer them. I'm the Sheikh's international legal advisor. That's all you need to know.'

'I'll be the judge of that, *cherie*,' he contradicted softly.

Laura met the formidable glint in his black eyes and suddenly some of her composure left her. 'We'll...we'll be landing soon.' And she couldn't wait. Being cooped up in here with him, with the tension growing by the second, was her idea of a nightmare.

Laura unsnapped her seat-belt and stood up, wanting to get away from the mesmerising spotlight of his stare and his increasingly probing questions.

Acutely aware of his eyes following her every move, she went over to one of the round porthole windows and stared down at where mountaintops were capped with snow which looked like thick white daubs of paint. Oh, please let's just get there, she thought.

'So what was the particular *talent* which made you the successful candidate for this job?' he murmured. 'Or can I guess?'

'I told you. I'm a lawyer—there are papers I need to witness.' She turned round to see that Xavier had also risen to his feet, and that his eyes were gleaming with something which was fast approaching menace.

'Don't play disingenuous,' he drawled. 'It doesn't suit you. There are a million lawyers out there who could have done the job, but none that look as good as you. Were you chosen for your beauty and your sex-appeal, do you think?'

Sex-appeal? Laura knew that the stylist had worked

an almost complete transformation on her physical appearance—but it was hard to change your own view of yourself. Because the mirror *could* lie—every woman knew that. How you looked had little to do with how you felt on the inside—particularly for someone who had fought insecurity all her life.

She had been the hand-to-mouth daughter of a hard-up mother and then the diligent law student. And latterly—with Josh—she had been frigid and uptight Laura, the cash-cow who had been laughably easy to milk and then send on her way. Yes, she was wearing a fortune in clothes—but sexy? Her? Never in a million years. Not according to Josh, anyway.

'Of course I wasn't!' she defended. 'I may have been chosen because women have different qualities to men, but my sex-appeal is not only irrelevant but inappropriate to a country like Kharastan.'

Was she really naïve enough to believe that? he wondered. He walked over to the window to stand beside her and looked down into her face, his eyes narrowing in perplexity as he saw that her green eyes were huge and dark in her white face.

Women did not usually shrink from him like this, and it was turning him on—deep down he wanted something or someone to lash out at for the unusual situation he unwillingly found himself in. And why should it not be her? Don't shoot the messenger, urged a voice inside his head, and Xavier's mouth tightened. *Ah, non*—he wasn't intending to *shoot* the messenger.

'So you reckon it's just some kind of coincidence that they should have appointed a nubile young woman to do the job?' he questioned, his voice edgy with desire.

'I don't know,' she whispered, as if she had suddenly come to realise the trap she found herself in. Backed up against the wall, ostensibly alone on a powerful jet with a powerful man whose whole large and muscular frame emanated a raw kind of sexuality. It shimmered from his skin in a hot, almost tangible radiance—so that despite knowing she should be distancing herself, or calling for the stewardess, Laura found herself curiously debilitated, unable to move, or to think, or to…

'Don't you?' he whispered back, and touched the tip of his finger to her chin, tilting it upwards and forcing her to meet the piercing black gaze. 'I think you do. Just as I think that someone told the Sheikh's entourage about those rosebud lips and knew that I would want to do this…'

He was lowering his face towards hers, and Laura felt like one of those women in a sci-fi film—zapped into compete immobility by some alien's ray-gun. Except it was nothing remotely alien which was freezing her to the spot—it was a feeling as old and human as creation itself, even though it had never hit her quite like this before. Xavier lowered his mouth down onto her trembling lips.

Perhaps if it had been a hard and blatant kiss—a demonstration of his superior power and experience—then Laura might have had the strength or the desire to push him away. But it wasn't. It was the cleverest kiss in the world, for it coaxed and hinted and tantalised and made her yearn for more. So that it was *her* mouth which parted slightly, and *her* tongue which gave a little flick towards his.

And *his* low laugh of triumph and anticipation as he placed his hands on her waist and then slid them down to cup her buttocks and draw her towards him, as he deepened the kiss with an instinctive display of sensuality and mastery.

'Mmm,' he murmured against her lips.

'Xavier!' she gasped.

'You like that?'

'Y…yes! Oh, *yes*!'

Xavier laughed again, tempted to cup her breasts, or to slide the long filmy dress up her long legs and explore her most secret treasures. But a hasty mental calculation told him that there was no time to enjoy any kind of sexual game. Starting something might mean that they were both left high and dry—or, worse, that they might be interrupted by the stewardess telling them that they were coming in to land.

No, there was no time for sex—but plenty of time for sexual promise. And it sure beat worrying about what lay ahead in Kharastan. Xavier knew how much value women placed on a kiss—how they played it over again and again in their minds, like a much-loved piece of music. Well, then, let her have the long, sweet kiss of all her romantic fantasies.

Using his mouth like an instrument, he continued to

explore her lips in soft and provocative caresses until, with a little cry, Laura reached up to cling onto his broad shoulders and began to sway slightly as the kiss became harder now, and deeper.

His lips tasted sweet, the sweetest thing she had ever tasted. Laura had been kissed before—of course she had—but never like this. Oh, never like this. She could feel the sticky rush of desire, the debilitating sense of wonder which made her want him to...to...

With a soft smile Xavier drew back from her, hearing her tiny moan of protest. He stared down into eyes which looked almost black, so dilated were her pupils, and her mouth was darkened too by his kiss. There was a faint flush accentuating her cheekbones—and he knew with arrogant certainty that if the flight had been just a little longer he would be having sex with her, right now.

'Alas, *non*,' he murmured regretfully, for he was so hard that he felt he might burst. 'There is no time for love, *cherie*.'

Was it his totally inappropriate use of the word 'love' which brought Laura crashing back to reality? Like someone who had been thrown from the confusing blackness of a cave into blinking light?

She took a tottering step back in complete and utter horror, her hand flying to her throat. 'Wh...what are you *doing*?' she breathed unsteadily, and then shook her head in disbelief. 'Or rather, what am *I* doing?'

He laughed. 'You want a biology lesson?'

'I want....I want.... Oh! How could I have been

so…*stupid*?' To let him kiss her like that—to open her body and her mouth up to him, telling him in no uncertain terms that for that brief moment she had wanted him in the most complete sense. How could she possibly play the cool lawyer *now*?

Xavier gave a lazy smile. 'Do not beat yourself up, *cherie*—it is no crime to want me. Most women do.' He shrugged. 'And what better way to pass the time during the long nights ahead in the desert?' To use sex as an escape from thought—ah, yes, it had many uses other than pleasure and procreation. 'We will make love just as soon as we get an opportunity to do so.'

Common sense splashed over Laura's senses like a cold shower at his arrogant sexual boast. Her hands flew up to her hair and she knew she must straighten it before they came into land—and, more importantly, that she must make it clear that there would be no repeat of what had just happened. None. No matter how provocatively he kissed her. *And you aren't going to let him do it again!*

'I don't think so. That was a very serious error of judgement on my part,' she said, her voice steadier now. 'One which will not be repeated—for once I have effected an introduction between you and the Sheikh then my dealings with you will be over, and I will bid you farewell.'

Xavier resisted the desire to contradict her. How little she knew! How naïve and foolish if she thought that he would allow such a scenario to take place. She would bid him farewell only when *he* had tired of her, and that would be not be until he had had her.

He felt a pulse beat deep within his groin.

Oh, yes—she would be his for the taking.

But sexual hunger was replaced with a different kind of tension as the sound of the jet engines changed and the plane began its descent into Kharastan.

CHAPTER FIVE

JUST a month earlier and Laura had made this very same landing, onto a runway fringed by huge and distant snow-topped mountains, and it had made her gasp aloud in wonder. But then she had been hopeful as well as nervous—filled with the kind of excitement you got when you were stepping outside of the confines of your normal world.

She had been slightly terrified of meeting the Sheikh's representative—but equally she had been feeling strong. The hurt and the subsequent fall-out she had experienced from the break-up of her relationship with Josh had somehow transformed itself into a brand-new attitude of resilience and defiance.

Most importantly, she had done everything in her power to extricate herself from the situation with something more than pride. She had seen her mother suffer financially at the hands of men, and she was determined not to repeat her mistakes. Yes, this time a month ago, life had looked hopeful.

And now?

Now she just felt the terror and none of the strength. It seemed to have been sapped by the sexy man who had kissed her with such unbearably sweet and restrained passion on the plane and left her aching and uncomfortable. And how unprofessional was *that*?

Laura shot him a glance as they stood at the top of the aircraft steps, watched his reaction as he breathed in his first breath of the warm Kharastan air which seemed to envelop her body like a warm caress. But she didn't want to think of being caressed, because that would take her mind to pointless places.

She wanted to feel something other than this prickly state of ebbing desire, and tried to concentrate on his high-handed arrogance instead. But somehow she couldn't seem to do it. His black eyes had narrowed as they took in his surroundings, and for a moment there seemed to be an almost unguarded air about him. Stupidly, it made her think about a little boy searching for his father and his roots—instead of a calculating playboy who knew how to kiss a woman in order to guarantee seduction—and, even more stupidly, she felt her heart turn over.

'Ready?' she questioned softly.

'Wait,' he said, his deep voice as soft as hers.

Xavier looked around him, as if excessive sound might disturb the natural quiet beauty of this place, and a peculiar sensation shivered over his skin as he stared out at a stunningly unfamiliar landscape.

The sun was beginning its slow descent in a clear sky

of intense cobalt, and it seemed a much bigger sun than the one he was used to—a gigantic, fiery ball of coppery red which was turning the snow on top of the distant mountains into pink cream.

He saw the dark shape of a huge bird swooping by him, and noticed the dust and the dry air and the heat which seemed to seep straight into his pores—and for a moment he felt utterly mesmerised by this strange new world.

He had grown up in a city, had lived and breathed an urban life since birth, and he loved Paris with a passion because it was impossible not to. Yes, he had travelled, but always more west than east, and his trips to the latter had been infrequent working trips to the highly populated finance capitals of the world. But this place looked wild and almost desolate, and it struck some deep, warm chord—made his heart lurch in a strange and unexpected way.

'*Mais c'est magnifique,*' he whispered.

'Yes,' said Laura slowly, and she stopped and caught the moment and just drank in the beauty. Magnificent indeed. And, under the guise of reaquainting herself with the landscape, she couldn't resist snatching another look at that strong and rugged profile—etched like a stark and beautiful portrait painting against the deep blue backdrop of the sky behind him. As if he was meant to be here. As if he belonged here. I wonder if he feels that too? she thought suddenly. Or whether it's just fanciful imagining on my part?

Xavier's gaze swept from the panoramic view to the

airport itself, where there were gleaming, state-of-the-art buildings and high-tech radar—as well as the control towers. But when his eyes had adjusted to the clear light he could see armed soldiers on the edge of the airfield, along with convoy of dark and gleaming vehicles and a number of motorcycle outriders.

'Here they come,' he observed softly, as a handful of people—all men—proceeded towards them, their silken robes and headdresses shimmering in the dying light of the sun.

Can this be for real? Xavier wondered. Or had he wandered onto a film set—where fantasy was cleverly designed to mimic reality? Yet had his whole world not been turned upside down within the space of a couple of short days?

'Which one is the Sheikh's special aide?' he questioned tersely.

Laura's eyes were raking over the granite-faced group. 'The tallest of them,' she said slowly. 'The man in the white robe. Malik.'

'And you say they are related?'

'Only very distantly, I believe—but he is definitely the Sheikh's confidante. He tells him everything.'

Xavier's eyes gleamed with satisfaction. And had she not answered as *his* confidante? He had been right—as usual—a taste of his sublime lovemaking had been enough to guarantee that all her loyalty would soon lie with *him*. It was time for him to take control. 'Come,' he ordered. 'Let us go and greet them.'

Laura blinked as he preceded her down the aeroplane steps, wondering whether Xavier had decided that he was going to start *acting* like a royal—for wasn't there something suddenly imperious in his manner?

And did she imagine the merest flicker of hostility in the eyes of Malik as he approached them, bowing deeply from the waist?

'Good evening,' he said formally. 'I, Malik—on behalf of His Most Eminent Highness Zahir of Kharastan—bid you welcome.'

A nerve flickered at Xavier's cheek. There was a part of him, a primitive part, that wanted to demand answers to a few incisive questions—to demand some kind of proof of the outrageous claim which had led to him being here on foreign soil. Something more than a damned black-and-white shot which could have been mocked up by any half-decent photographer! But it was not Malik's story to tell.

Instead, he nodded his jet-dark head in response. 'I thank you for your extravagant welcome,' he answered silkily.

'You must be tired, and thirsty after your journey,' said Malik. 'The car awaits to take us to the Palace.' He turned to Laura. 'You will take the first car, where you will find Sidonia, your maidservant, awaits you,' he instructed. 'Monsieur de Maistre and I will follow in the other.'

His voice was definitely cool, and Laura suddenly felt as if the men were closing ranks and excluding her. She had achieved what they had asked her to do—did that mean she was now superfluous to requirements?

I don't *want* to travel in a separate car with a servant, she thought—flicked away as you would an irritating fly on a hot summer's day. She turned to look at Xavier, but his eyes were stony and his face unmoving—the man who had kissed her so passionately on the plane now seemed like a distant dream. Would he object to this sudden segregation of the sexes? she wondered. Would his obvious desire for her go as far as wanting her companionship on the journey to the Palace?

Xavier met her eyes. He knew that she wanted to stay with him—and, in truth, would he not have preferred her beside him? Familiar and beautiful. But her beauty was distracting—and not just to him. He wanted to keep all his wits about him—and, like a small animal locked outside in the cold and rain—her gratitude would know no bounds when he took her back into the warmth of his arms once more. Let her have a taste of what it was like to be rejected by Xavier de Maistre, and in future she would acquiesce to his every desire!

Besides, Laura and Malik both had the potential to be his enemy, and was it not best to divide your enemies? So that if necessary you could play one off against the other…?

'Run along now, *cherie*,' he murmured. 'As you see—everyone is ready to leave.'

Laura didn't react—even though his patronising dismissal felt like a slap to the face. Yet she had travelled out here before under her own steam and managed admirably—because she had been playing her professional role instead of allowing a passionate kiss to knock her guard down. So start playing it again! You are here as an employee, she reminded herself, and nothing more.

She nodded and gave a serene smile. 'Yes, of course. You men will have plenty to talk about. I'll see you at the Palace.' And she turned and walked towards the car without another word, knowing that they watched her.

For a moment both men were silent as a guard sprang to attention and opened the door of the armoured car for her.

'She is beautiful, is she not?' asked Malik reflectively.

Xavier turned his head back to look at the Sheikh's aide, acknowledging the glint in the other's eyes with a stony response. Had this man already been intimate with the luscious redhead? he wondered. And a dart of sexual jealousy lanced right through him. 'Laura?'

'Of course,' said Malik, and then paused. 'She is your lover?' he questioned deliberately.

A furrow appeared between Xavier's black eyebrows. 'Is it the custom in Kharastan to speak of women in such a way?' he demanded.

Malik acknowledged the barb with a slight shrug. 'You come from the West—where attitudes towards sex are liberal, and where your own reputation with women is that of a legendary stud.'

'And where only schoolboys boast to each other of sexual conquests,' returned Xavier.

'I was not asking you to boast—I was merely trying

to find out whether Miss Cottingham has yet joined the long list of your lovers.'

'My *reputed* lovers,' drawled Xavier. 'If I had bedded all the women who have offered themselves to me then there would be little time for anything else.'

'So is that a yes or a no?' persisted Malik.

Xavier's eyes narrowed. Was it just masculine pride which made him reluctant to admit that Laura had not yet been his, since the Sheikh's aide was clearly obsessed with her? Or was it a niggling doubt that perhaps she actually might do the unthinkable and resist him? Never! There was not a woman born who was foolish enough to deny herself *that*.

Think about the way she responded to you on the flight over, he told himself, offering a tantalising fore-taste of the abundant pleasures to come. 'You display a curiosity on the subject which borders on the distaste-ful,' he gritted.

Malik shrugged. 'Perhaps I am thinking of sleeping arrangements.'

'Or perhaps you want her for yourself?' Xavier chal-lenged. 'Tell me—is it necessary for you to employ a woman to be able to take her to your bed?'

There was a moment of disbelieving silence. 'Your comments could be construed as insults, Monsieur de Maistre,' observed Malik coldly. 'Is that wise, do you think?'

But Xavier refused to be cowed by the menace which had suddenly crept into the other man's voice. I don't *have* to like this man, or respect or pay homage to him, he thought. 'If I were being wise, then I probably wouldn't have agreed to come on this damned journey in the first place!'

'Then why did you?'

Xavier's lips curved into a glacial smile. 'I will talk to the Sheikh,' he said carelessly. 'And not to one of his henchmen.'

He saw that his incautious words had made Malik clench his fists in the folds of his silken robes in ill-disguised fury—and suddenly Xavier felt almost *reckless*. As if he had just been given a draught of cool refreshment after being parched and dry for longer than he cared to remember. Before him lay a gilded path to the unknown, and suddenly that excited him—because for all his freedom and his many glittering successes hadn't his life become just a little *predictable*?

After all, there were only so many fine wines you could drink, exquisite meals you could eat and beautiful women you could bed. When you wore nothing but silk or cashmere or Irish linen next to your skin, when every whim and wish was granted—did you not lose something of the fierce hunter which lay at the deepest core of every man?

A luxurious palate could grow jaded, but for the first time in as long as he could remember Xavier's blood began to fizz with an elemental excitement as the car drove down a wide avenue, where rows of guards saluted as they passed.

He sighted an ornate set of metal gates—turned blood-red by the dying embers of the sun. Through them he could see a glimpse of water, spraying up in a white plume from a huge fountain, and unknown trees throwing down dark and dappled shadows onto immaculate paths.

As they approached the compound he could see a domed building covered in exquisite mosaic and the glint of gold. Alongside the gold was blue of every shade imaginable—from summer sky to ocean deep.

And, despite his unfamiliar heightened state of emotion, Xavier suddenly felt a strange and powerful sense of destiny—as if it was his place to be here, now.

'We are here,' he observed slowly, and saw Malik had been quietly watching him, an unfathomable look in black eyes so like his own.

'Indeed we are,' said the Kharastan man softly. 'The Blue Palace is very beautiful, yes? And it is here that Zahir the Great awaits you.'

Zahir the Great. *The man who claims to be my...father,* Xavier thought, and then a strange sense of isolation crept over him. What if none of it were true? What if this strange, almost dream-like state turned out to be exactly that?

Because—for all his money and his power and connections—Zahir might have made a fundamental mistake: the kind all men were capable of. It might turn out to be some random error—and then what?

Xavier must be very careful indeed not to allow his

customary cool composure to slip. To remain as indifferent as he always did—because he would be watched closely for his reactions, and an unguarded moment could be interpreted as weakness. And that he would *never* allow.

'When will I see him?' he questioned suddenly.

There was a pause. 'It has not yet been decided,' said Malik.

Xavier could sense the other man's authority reasserting itself, and he knew that he must demonstrate his own power.

Because they want you here far more than you want to be here, he reminded himself.

'I have travelled out here at considerable inconvenience—and I will not be left dangling like a puppet on a string,' he asserted fiercely. 'If Sheikh Zahir wishes to see me, then so be it—but it must be accomplished as quickly as possible. I am a busy man who does not play to another's whims.'

Malik's eyes became stony. 'It is not a game that we play with you, Frenchman,' he grated. 'Zahir is old and frail and the time of your meeting will be governed by the state of his health—by that, and that alone.'

Xavier's heard the raw note which had distorted Malik's voice, and his eyes narrowed. Was he genuinely fond of his master, in the way that sometimes happened with a subordinate? he wondered. Or was he just projecting into a future without the Sheikh and worrying about his own livelihood?

But he looked into the other man's eyes and saw genuine grief there, and it smote at Xavier's conscience. 'I did not intend to cause you pain,' he grated.

Malik inclined his head in thanks and appeared to regain his composure. 'Obviously, the meeting will be arranged as soon as possible.'

There were a million questions teeming in Xavier's mind—but now was not the time to ask them.

Malik's voice broke into his thoughts.

'Dinner will be at nine, after you and Miss Cottingham have had a chance to refresh yourselves. I hope that will meet with your approval?'

And suddenly Xavier knew that he wanted—needed—to assert himself in other ways, too. To follow up on the promise of his kiss with the beautiful Englishwoman. Because what else was he going to do with the idle hours while he waited for the Sheikh to see him? 'What *will* meet with my approval is if the sleeping arrangements are to my satisfaction,' he said, with soft, smooth emphasis.

Malik stiffened. 'That depends on what you mean by *satisfaction*.'

'I think we both know what I mean,' said Xavier softly.

There was a moment's silence. 'Obviously it would greatly offend Kharastan sensibilities if two unmarried people were openly put in the same room, but...' Malik shrugged his shoulders and a knowing look passed between the two men. 'I am certain that something can be arranged to your satisfaction.'

'I'm glad we understand each other,' said Xavier.

CHAPTER SIX

'I THINK there must have been some kind of mistake!' declared Laura, as she looked around the room with a mixture of anger, fear and unquestionable excitement.

'Mistake?' echoed Xavier innocently as two servants put down the last of their bags. 'And what kind of mistake would that be, *cherie*?'

'Sharing a suite!' she declared. 'With *you*!'

She was glaring at him as if he was devil himself, and Xavier allowed a feeling of brief contentment to wash over him. How much easier to allow his thoughts to be dominated by the familiar frission of sexual tension rather than wondering about the wisdom of having come here on such a strange quest.

'Well, it isn't exactly *sharing*, is it, *cherie*? We have one sitting room in common—surely you can deal with that for a few nights?' He raised his black brows in mocking query. 'Did you never share with members of the opposite sex when you were a law student?'

'That's *different*!'

'How is it different, Laura?'

'Playing the innocent doesn't suit you, Xavier,' she said. 'Are you behind this?'

'Behind what?'

'The fact that we're going to be virtually living on top of one another!'

His dark, sensual face now assumed an expression of faint perplexity. 'You think that the possibility of my being the Sheikh's illegitimate son means that I have been able to wield control, perhaps even from France? What did you imagine, Laura—that I somehow managed to acquire a direct line to Zahir and demand that he put us in close proximity?'

'So you *didn't* have anything to do with it? Was that a yes or a no?'

Ah, *oui*—she was clever; he would give her that. Or maybe it was her lawyer's training, seeing straight through his elaborately bluffed response and realising that he hadn't actually answered her question.

'Is it such a bad arrangement?' he questioned, gesturing around the cool, shaded room, with its stone floors and priceless silk rugs in faded jewel colours. There was a glorious bureau, inlaid with many different gleaming woods, and on it stood a vase of sweetly scented roses. 'It is a beautiful room—in fact, it is so large that it could easily be divided into three rooms. And what is there to complain about when we have been given separate bedrooms?'

'Except that there aren't any keys in the locks, are

there?' she pointed out. And he still hadn't answered her question.

'Really? I hadn't got around to checking that.' He raised his dark brows and gave an arrogant laugh. 'Do you think that a locked door would keep me out if I really wanted to get into your bedroom?'

Laura's heart missed a beat. 'You don't mean you'd *break the door down*?' she questioned in a faint voice.

'Why? Is that one of your abiding fantasies?'

'No!'

'What I meant,' he murmured, noting the automatic way her pupils had dilated and feeling an answering stir of desire, 'was that if I wished it, then you would turn the key and let me in.'

'Are you crazy?' She stared at him. 'Do you live in the kind of world where women just fall in with your every whim?'

Their eyes met. 'Pretty much.'

Laura shook her head. 'You treat women like sexual objects,' she complained.

'Which they are.'

'I can't believe you said that!'

'Because it is true,' he mused, enjoying the verbal sparring for its rarity value as much as for a distraction. 'Your objection is in the wording—and all the associations which have grown up around it. When a man looks at a beautiful woman he thinks of sex—but it works both ways. Women think the same way about men—if only they would have the courage to admit it.' He slanted her a shamelessly provocative look from beneath his thick black lashes. 'You were thinking about just that on the plane today.'

For once Laura was momentarily speechless. The trouble was that she couldn't fault his logic, his cleverness with words. He would have made a good lawyer himself, she thought reluctantly. 'Well, maybe I'll ask Malik to change my room.'

'You could try,' he said softly. 'But perhaps it might be a waste of your time—and time is so precious, is it not?'

Their eyes met, and in that moment Laura understood. 'Oh, I see,' she said. 'So I was right—you *were* behind it. It's a *fait accompli.*'

'How perfect your French accent it,' he murmured. He let his gaze drift over her. And how perfect *she* looked, he thought—that creamy silk providing a gloriously neutral backdrop against which to appreciate her natural beauty.

Her dark red hair had been drawn back from the perfect oval of her face and woven into an intricate kind of plait, which began at the top of her head. Yet its almost severe style contrasted with the luscious hint of curves beneath the soft silk, and he welcomed the familiar leap of sexual hunger which silenced all the clamouring questions in his mind.

How many men had known that exquisite body? he wondered jealously, remembering Malik's casual questioning in the car. *Then have her,* mocked a voice in his head. *Have her and then you can forget all about her.*

'Do you never wear your hair down?' he questioned softly.

It wasn't what Laura had been expecting. She had seen the hungry way his eyes had been devouring her, and she had anticipated some sensual little taunt, steeling herself against the seduction of his words. But his sensual question made her feel just that. Her fingertips touched the carefully crafted style, skating over the slippery silken surface of the thick dark red locks.

'Sometimes I do,' she said.

'In bed?'

Don't let him get to you. Don't give him any inkling that you keep remembering the sweetness of his kiss... She saw the hectic glimmer in his black eyes and realised that he was remembering it, too. And that the greatest victory would be not to get herself moved from the temptations of an interjoining room—but to resist temptation altogether.

'Of course I let my hair down in bed,' she said briskly. 'But you won't ever get to see it, Xavier.'

He gave her a hard, swift smile. 'Don't you know that a red-blooded man can never resist a challenge?' he murmured, flicking a quick glance at his watch. 'And—while you look utterly delectable as you are—you might wish to change before dinner.'

He walked into his bedroom and shut the door with an exaggerated sense of care, leaving Laura staring after him with a growing sense of frustration which was more than sexual. As if he had just got the better of her and she wasn't quite sure why.

Outside, the stars hung bright and brilliant in the indigo velvet of the sky—as big as if a child had painted them on with large brushstrokes. And drifting into the room was warm, soft air—heavily scented with the fragrance of roses and jasmine and sandalwood.

She walked slowly into her own bedroom and closed the door. She should have been bouncing around with satisfaction, feeling *good* about herself, and yet she was all churned up. Was that because Xavier was managing to unsettle her? Or because she was terrified of the way he was making her feel, and even more terrified of the way she suspected he *could* make her feel?

Laura sighed. Just make the most of this opportunity, she told herself. Banish the Frenchman from your mind and enjoy the experience of staying as a guest in a real-life palace. Not many Western women get this kind of chance. She thought of how her mother would marvel if she could see her little girl now—her sweet mother, who seemed to attract chaos and never had a penny in her purse without wanting to spend it.

Within the hour, Laura felt like a different person. The palace might have dated back to the fourteenth century, but the bathrooms were most definitely rooted in the twenty-first—with powerful showerheads as big as dinner plates and a stand-alone bath you could practically swim in.

She applied the minimum of make-up and slithered into a fitted dress in deepest jade silk, which skimmed her ankles and brought out the deep green of her eyes. Then she pulled her hair back into a chignon to give her finished image a rather defiant look.

Drawing in a deep breath, she opened the interconnecting door to find Xavier standing looking out at a huge crescent moon. He turned round when he heard her, and for one immeasurable moment they both stood staring at each other, like two people who had stumbled over each other by mistake.

Xavier stilled, feeling the sudden deep pounding of his heart. She had no flesh on show, save for her face, and yet he had never seen anyone look more sexy in his life. How did she do that touch/don't-touch thing so beautifully? he wondered. He had been aching when he had gone to take his shower and had been tempted to pleasure himself…and now he wished he had.

'You look beautiful.'

Stupidly, she felt her lips tremble. 'Xavier, please don't.'

'Don't what?'

'Don't *say* those things.' *Don't look at me that way!*

'All men say those things.'

'No, they don't.' *Not like you do.*

'You want me to lie, is that it? Because I will not. And you are. Very beautiful.'

Laura felt a glow suffusing her skin as his words whispered over her—because when he looked at her in that lazily appreciative way he made her *feel* beautiful. But it wasn't right to conduct a flirtation with him—under any circumstances, and especially under ones such as these.

Even though Xavier seemed unconvinced that the Sheikh was his father, Laura was pretty sure he was. And very soon he was going to meet him. Already their worlds were miles apart—he was a wealthy playboy and Laura was a small-town lawyer from another country—but add a royal connection into the equation and he would be completely out of her reach. So keep resisting him, she told herself fiercely. Keep yourself safe from his Gallic charm and his dark, sexy looks.

In the distance, a sonorous bell was rung, its chime sweet and low and long, just as someone tapped on the door and an unknown male servant in plain white robes bowed and indicated that they should follow him.

Instinctively, Laura glanced up at Xavier.

'Are you…nervous?' she ventured.

Usually he would have deflected her observation with a cold indignation that she should dare suggest that Xavier de Maistre should be nervous of anything! But tonight he did not. Maybe it was the scent of sandalwood on the air, or the crescent moon in the sky, but tonight he did not feel like the Xavier of old.

'Not at all,' he murmured, as they passed tall marble pillars and intricate fretwork lamps which hung down from a jewelled ceiling. 'I feel a little as if I am surrendering to the inevitable—but to something which is nothing to do with me.'

'I don't think I understand.'

'None of this matters,' he said slowly, as if he was making sense of it to himself as well as to her. 'If—which I question—the Sheikh *does* happen to be my father, then it is merely an accident of birth. Nature's random lottery. It is not part of my life. It never has been and it never will be, nor can be.'

'Are you sure?'

But her question went unanswered, for by now they were approaching a vast set of ornately carved double doors which were thrown open upon first sight of them.

Inside, he could see torches of fire set out at intervals around a vast room with an ornate table at its centre, on which glittered precious crystal and silver with tall, ivory candles amid fruit and flowers. *'Mon dieu,'* he murmured. 'Look at this.'

Xavier glanced down at Laura but she was not looking at the lavishly set banqueting hall. Instead her face was turned to up his in question, the green eyes clear but curious—as soothing as a smooth green lake—and he found himself wanting to dive in and lose himself.

'Did your mother ever talk about your father?' she asked suddenly.

Had the enchantment of an Eastern night worked some of its magic on him? Was that why he didn't shoot her down in flames for her impertinance? 'You have no right to ask me something like that, Laura.'

'Don't I?' she retorted softly. 'Considering we're sharing living space, I'd say that gives me a few rights.'

She was tenacious, he would say that for her—and brave too, to pursue a subject which he found uncomfortable. And if she had the courage to ask him, then surely he had the courage to answer? Yet it was strange to give voice to thoughts he had always repressed—partly because there had never been anyone in whom to confide before. But Laura knew most of the story—so why not answer her?

'My mother said next to nothing about my father,' Xavier answered, his black eyes as hard and impenetrable as jet. 'His identity was the secret she carried closest to her heart. All I knew was that he was rich and powerful and potentially acquisitive. But he had no part in our lives, not even in anecdotes…' He clicked his fingers, like a sorcerer demonstrating someone disappearing in a puff of smoke. 'It was as though he was dead to her—as though he never existed.'

As though he never existed.

It was a damning and terrible testimony passed down from mother to child, and neither of them spoke for a moment—as if his stark words had robbed them both of the power of speech.

'Maybe you'll hate him,' said Laura suddenly. *And then what?* Had Malik—or Xavier—or even the Sheikh himself—thought about the possible consequences of that happening?

The scent of jasmine wafted through the air as they walked towards the entrance to the hall. 'Maybe I will,' agreed Xavier in an odd kind of voice.

CHAPTER SEVEN

'YOU will perhaps eat a little more dessert?' asked Malik softly.

Laura shook her head as an ornate golden dish, gleaming black and scarlet with grapes and pomegranates, was presented to her by one of the many silent servers at the meal.

She sat back in her chair. This was the only official Kharastan function she had attended, yet the evening was proving far less of an ordeal than she might have imagined, given that she was seated next to the flinty-faced Malik, with Xavier on the opposite side of the table.

'Thank you, but, no—I couldn't eat another thing.'

'You enjoyed it? I think perhaps it was a little plain for your sophisticated Western palate.'

'Are you kidding?' asked Laura. 'A night out where I live usually involves a trip to the cinema followed by a curry. But this was different—and I loved everything about it. The dancers were incredible. Obviously I couldn't understand a word of the poetry, but it had

such a wonderful rhythm that it didn't seem to matter—
and the music which accompanied it was beautiful.'

'Yes,' said Malik, looking pleased. 'All good poetry
transcends language. And the flute you so admired—the
sound it produces sounds exactly like the wind blowing
across the desert, does it not? Ah, I see you frowning!
Have you ever been in the desert, Miss Cottingham?'

'No, I haven't,' said Laura, her eyes drifting across
and down the table, to where Xavier was sitting talking
to a beautiful Kharastani woman garbed in lavishly embroidered robes, with filigree earrings of sapphire and
gold hanging from her ears. Did he find the woman
attractive? she found herself wondering jealously.

He chose just that moment to look up—or had he
sensed her staring at him? His lips curved into a mocking
half-smile and his eyes flashed with promise as they
lazily ran over her face. Laura felt her throat tighten. She
folded her fingers in the soft jade silk at her lap, aware
that they were trembling and wondering how the hell she
was going to cope later. When they were alone.

Malik's eyes followed her gaze. 'The guests here
tonight are old and trusted confidantes of the royal
household, and Fallalah is married to one of the Sheikh's
many godsons,' he said obliquely as small teacups were
placed before them. 'Just in case her chatter with the
Frenchman should give you any cause for concern.'

Laura blinked as she dragged her gaze away from
Xavier. 'Concern?' she said, clearing her throat. 'Why
should there be?'

'Forgive me,' said Malik slickly. 'But I thought perhaps that you and he were…' He shrugged and let his voice trail off, the pause giving rise to a hundred silent questions.

It was a clever way of eliciting information, Laura acknowledged—but she was damned if she was going to start discussing her relationship with Xavier. She smiled to herself. And what relationship would that be? A man who made no pretence about wanting sex with her, and a woman who told herself that it would be wrong, no matter how much her body tried to persuade her otherwise. Not much of a relationship!

'You're speaking in riddles, Malik.'

'Am I? Forgive me.'

Laura nodded, but said nothing in response.

'So you are discreet,' Malik observed. 'And loyal.'

'Wasn't that why you employed me—for those very qualities?' Laura folded her napkin and, placing it neatly on the table, looked up at him. 'Maybe it's time we talked about that. I know you want me to witness the signing of some documents, and I can do that first thing.' Her gaze was steady, hopeful. 'After I've done that can I assume that my job is completed, as I will have accomplished everything you asked me to do?'

The Kharastani nobleman took a white grape from the dish and turned it in his olive fingers reflectively. 'As I recall, when you were interviewed you were told that more work could be available on completion of this assignment and depending on its outcome.'

Laura shifted in her seat. What tricks the light could play, she thought. Tonight, in the guttering light from the candles, she thought how much Malik's jet-black eyes seemed to resemble Xavier's. Or was her perception simply being warped by the travel and the upheaval and the sheer mind-blowing beauty of the Blue Palace and this heady evening?

'Well, the work *is* nearly completed,' Laura said softly.

'No,' he demurred. 'It is completed when the Sheikh instructs that it is so.'

'And when will that be? Days? Weeks?' With the two of them thrown together in the most bizarre and intimate circumstances in the meantime. As Laura looked into Malik's eyes she realised that he was as ruthless as Xavier. What he wanted, he got—and behind the outward courtesy she had been shown tonight she could read the implacable determination in his eyes. She was here to stay until she was given leave to go, as simple as that.

At that moment Malik turned his head and looked towards the door, just as a slim young woman entered the room. She wore a light-blue gown and was veiled, but Laura couldn't help noticing the gleam of pure blonde hair beneath it, and her pale, clear skin. Her overall appearance was positively medieval, and Laura watched as her blue eyes sought out Malik, giving him one brief but definite nod of her head, before quietly slipping out of the same door she'd entered by.

'Who is that?' Laura asked.

There was a pause. 'Her name is Sorrel.'

'She doesn't look like a Kharistani.'

'No. She is English, and she is my ward.'

'Your *ward*?'

'You sound surprised, Miss Cottingham.'

'A little. It's an old-fashioned term which doesn't get used very much in England these days.' But it seemed to match the girl's old-world appearance—redolent of a time when women needed to be placed under the care of a guardian.

'We are an old-fashioned country,' said Malik carefully. 'And we protect our women. Sorrel's parents are dead, but her family has for many years had ties with Kharastan. And she is very close to the Sheikh,' said Malik. 'In fact, I understand that his Supreme Highness is now ready to receive the Frenchman.'

Malik was rising to his feet and summoning one of the servants to his side. He bent his head and uttered something in his native tongue, and Laura watched the servant go round to speak to Xavier.

'You will excuse me?' questioned Malik. 'Someone will show you back to your quarters.'

'Thank you.'

He bent his dark head and spoke in a low voice, so that Laura had to strain her ears to hear him. 'In case it interests you, there is a key which fits your door, should you require it. You will find it in the small box made from mulberry in your dressing room. You will also find alcoholic beverages in the large bureau in the sitting room. You see, we cater for honoured Western guests even if many of us do not share their tastes. I will bid you goodnight, Miss Cottingham,' he added mockingly.

'Goodnight,' said Laura faintly, looking in surprise at his retreating figure. Had Malik just offered her the modern-day equivalent of protecting her honour? *We protect our women*, he had said earlier.

She saw Xavier rise to his feet, his face as unmoving as if it had been carved from a piece of granite, his mouth hard and his eyes cold, yet her heart went out to him, despite his forbidding look. Because surely deep down he *was* a little apprehensive? He might be a billionaire playboy but he was still only human—and how would anyone feel if they were on their way to find out if an ancient and powerful ruler was really their father?

She watched him and Malik leave the room together, as if they were compatriots of old, with none of the visible tension which had existed between them earlier.

So was it protectiveness which had made Malik tell her about the key—or was he just determined to make it as difficult as possible for the Frenchman to take a lover while he was here?

She bit her lip as Xavier's mocking boast came back to her:

Do you think that a locked door would keep me out?

Back in her room, she washed and undressed by the light of an ornate lamp which threw delicate shadows onto the silken rugs. Then she took out all the pins constraining her thick hair and, once it had fallen free, pulled on a soft silk nightgown.

But Laura could not sleep, even though the low divan with its crisp linen sheets was cool and inviting. She kept thinking about Xavier and wondering what was happening with him and Zahir. Eventually she admitted defeat, getting up to open the shutters of her window which looked out onto the Palace gardens—and the view she beheld was simply breathtaking.

Washed silver-white by moonlight, a wide path led down to a lake which was lined with perfectly trimmed shrubs. From here she could make out the scent of unknown flowers and feel the faint breeze which shimmered the leaves and her hair. This could have been Versailles or Hampton Court—or any of the famous palace gardens which had been designed on a lavish scale. Only the dark, gliding shape of the occasional bird of prey overhead reminded Laura that—although man could control his environment to some extent—this was a much wilder land than the one she was used to.

Minutes ticked by as she sat there, and eventually she heard the sound of an outer door being opened, and then closed again. Laura held her breath as if she was waiting—but waiting for what? To see if Xavier would knock, perhaps?

But there was no knock. She heard careful movements of shutters being pushed open, as if someone was trying very hard not to make a noise, and then nothing but silence—and yet more silence.

Xavier had clearly gone to bed, and she ought to think about doing the same—but her throat was parched dry by the air-conditioning. She would slip next door and fetch herself a cool drink—maybe that would help.

Pulling on a silk-satin robe which matched the negligee beneath, and knotting it tightly at the waist, Laura walked through into the sitting room. At first she didn't notice the dark figure silhouetted against the spangled sky, silent and unmoving as a statue—at least not until it moved, like a character on stage coming to life. Laura gave a little cry of alarm.

Xavier turned round, but his face was so shadowed that it was impossible to read what was there. But even if the sun had been overhead would Laura have known what was going on his mind? Or would his features be as tightly shuttered as they had been when he had walked out of the lavish banqueting hall with Malik earlier?

The sight of a half-naked woman following straight on from his meeting with the Sheikh was one stimulation too many, and the reality of her luscious breasts pushing against the silk of her robe set Xavier's pulse hammering and his already confused thoughts into overdrive.

'What the hell are you doing in here?' he demanded.

'I couldn't sleep.'

He stepped away from the windows into the room, and the light from the lamp showed a cold, hard look in his eyes.

'Well, try,' he instructed harshly. 'Because you certainly won't manage it standing up, looking at me.'

Looking like that. Like the answer to every man's aching dream. 'What are you doing here?' he snapped. 'After all the damned fuss you made earlier about sharing did you then decide you would like to tantalise me by drifting in here during the dead of night, dressed in next to nothing?'

'It's not next to nothing and I didn't know you were still awake!' she retorted. 'I wanted a drink of water, that's all!'

'So get one!' he bit back.

This was a different Xavier. Laura could see the sharp tension which was tightening his rugged features—even if she hadn't heard it distorting his voice. The skin seemed to be stretched tightly over his face, and she could see a muscle working frantically in his cheek. All that pressure building up inside him—wouldn't he explode if he didn't let it out?

Stupidly, Laura found herself wanting to stroke the tangled softness of his black hair as his tactiturn attitude made her heart soften. To hear him lashing out defensively like that surely meant that on some level he had been affected by what he had heard tonight. Because— for all his wealth and his influence and the women who adored him—Laura suddenly recognised that tonight the powerful playboy was completely alone in the world.

And why should you care?

'Would you like a drink?' she questioned, ignoring the mocking question in her head and telling herself it was only because no one could fail to be affected by the bleak expression in his eyes.

'Not water, and no more of those damned melon cocktails I had to endure during dinner. I could do with a real drink, if you must know.' His eyes narrowed as he watched her move like a dream across the room towards a polished cabinet made of walnut and apricot wood. 'What are you doing?'

'Getting you a drink.'

'I just told you—I don't *want* a soft drink.'

'That's not what I meant—there's some alcohol here. Malik told me.' Laura pulled open the door of the cabinet to reveal an assortment of bottles and different sizes of glass. 'I feel a little bit like the fairy godmother waving her wand,' she said. Surely you mean Cinderella? mocked the voice in her head. She looked up at him. 'What would you like? Wine? Beer? Champagne?'

'Not champagne,' he said flatly.

So we're not celebrating a paternal reunion, thought Laura. She pulled out a bottle of Kharastani wine and held it up. 'Shall we try this?'

'Why not?' He took the bottle from her without a word and poured the almost black liquid into two crystal glasses, glad to have the distraction of action. 'God knows what we're drinking,' he observed wryly. 'Kharastani wines aren't exactly a must-have for every good cellar.'

Laura accepted a glass from him and sipped it. It was thick, sweet and quite strong—and maybe that's just what he needs, she thought. Maybe just what *I* need. 'Gosh! That's strong.'

'You like it?'

'I can taste liquorice and something sweet.' Laura stared at him. 'But we've said everything there is to say about the wine—are you going to tell me what the Sheikh said to you?' *Whether he really is who he says he is and whether you have accepted that?*

Xavier took a mouthful of the liqueur-like drink and winced, then ran his tongue over lips suddenly grown dry. 'I guess that if I were in your situation I'd be curious, too.'

Very curious, thought Laura. She sat on one of the divans and looked up at him expectantly. 'What's he like?'

There was a pause. 'He's *old*,' he said flatly, and then shrugged. He looked up to see that her face was completely calm, as if someone had wiped every emotion away other than genuine concern.

'You wanted him to be strong and virile—a man in his prime—a man you could relate to?' she hazarded.

He shook his dark head. 'Of course I didn't. On an intellectual level I knew he'd be old—just not quite *that* old. I'm thirty-three and he's over eighty. He was nearly thirty years older than my mother!'

'Is that such a big deal? In Hollywood terms, it's nothing.'

'In France it is nothing either,' he lanced back, aware that he was not thinking rationally. 'But perhaps such a gap hits you hardest when you see the reality for the first time in old age.' Had it made him aware of his own life—and how quickly the years were passing?

She heard the edge to his voice. 'You're angry,' she observed.

'Yes, I am angry,' he agreed hotly. 'So what?'

'You ought to decide what it is you're angry about.'

His mouth twisted. 'Since when did lawyers start specialising in amateur psychology?'

'Have people spent their whole lives agreeing with you, Xavier?' she demanded. 'Or is it just that you can't bear to think someone else might have a different opinion which might just be right?'

He was taken aback by her straightforwardness, and more affected than he wanted to be by the compassion in her emerald eyes. Xavier had thought that he had grown a careful immunity to feelings, yet it was now clear that he had not. Was it a crime to concede that the whole experience had shaken him more than he would have thought possible? Or would anyone else have felt the same in the circumstances?

'Maybe,' he conceded, and met the question in her eyes. 'It's a story as old as time itself,' he said slowly. 'My mother was a young actress in Paris when the Sheikh first laid eyes on her. Zahir said that she had fire and passion and ambition in her heart.' His voice hardened. 'Which presumably is one of the things which drew him to her.'

'And presumably she was very beautiful?'

'Oh, she was beautiful,' he said flatly. 'She was exquisite.'

'So what happened?' asked Laura.

'They had an affair.'

'Secret?'

'*Mais, bien sûr.* Of course. He was a married man. And a high-profile one.'

'And...then what?'

Uncharacteristically, Xavier hesitated. The look in the Sheikh's eyes had spoken of regret—but was that the ruefulness of a man coming to the end of his life who looked back with wistfulness as he remembered the long-past pleasures of the flesh? Or was it genuine regret that he had abandoned a woman who was in love with him, without ever thinking that there might have been consequences to their ill-fated affair?

'Zahir came back to Kharastan,' he said slowly. 'And never saw her nor spoke to her again.'

'So he wouldn't acknowledge you as his son?'

Xavier looked at her, an odd note stealing into his voice. 'That's the strangest thing of all. He never knew about me—or so he claims,' he said. 'He only discovered my existence a couple of years ago, when he was trying to put his affairs in order. My photo had been seen by his aide in one of the French newspapers,' he said wryly. 'And the resemblance between us was pointed out to him. How ironic that he was prepared to be convinced by the evidence of a photo while I was not.'

'So what was it that finally convinced you that he *is* your father?' asked Laura quietly.

He could tell her that it was something he'd felt, something in his gut which was bone-deep and primitive, but that would be an admission too far for a man who rejected instinct—who relied on the infinitely safer world of fact and evidence.

Putting his hand into the pocket of his trousers, he withdrew a small object and placed it in the palm of his hand, where it gleamed in the moonlight. 'I brought it with me from Paris,' he said. 'It was all my mother left me—apart from a faded piece of ribbon.'

'What is it?' she whispered.

Xavier walked over to the divan and held his hand out, and Laura took it with trembling fingers. It was a ring of gold, with a stone she thought might be a ruby, though it was difficult to tell in the moonlight, and it was set like a star.

'Zahir has one exactly the same,' he said. 'It is very precious, and the gift of this ring is rarely made.'

'Which means your mother must really have meant something to him—do you think she knew that?'

He shrugged. 'Who knows?' He doubted it. She had been too busy struggling to survive and trying to hide her son from a man who could have helped her. Had he inherited his mistrust of others from her example? he suddenly found himself wondering.

'Maybe it was easier for her that way,' he said slowly. 'Because if you think someone cares it's all too easy to keep a dream alive—no matter how hopeless it is.'

Laura put her glass down. 'She never tried to tell him?'

Xavier shook his head, knowing that it would have been easy to shift the blame to his mother, for having denied him a father and having inculcated him with fear. But with the benefit of age and experience he could see now why she had acted as she had.

'He had no legitimate heir of his own in a land where male supremacy is unquestioned,' he said. 'Perhaps she was frightened that if he learned of my existence he might exercise his vast power to try to take me away from her. Presumably that was why she kept her own family in the dark, too—for fear that someone else might be persuaded to tell him. That was why she simply "disappeared", and we lived our strange life in the shadows, poor as church mice.'

'Poor?' asked Laura. surprised.

Xavier gave the ghost of a laugh. '*Oui, cherie,* poor—I was not born wealthy, you know. But we lived well—with food on the table and a fire at the grate.' Yet he recognised now the lasting legacy of his upbringing. Had the struggle and the secrecy of their lives been the driving force behind his need to acquire enough personal wealth for a million lifetimes, without acquiring any emotional baggage along the way?

'So why did he want to see you? And why now?'

'Because his wife died last year and that gave him the freedom to act—to tie up all the loose ends in his life. He felt that as long as the Sheikha was alive, it would be distressing to confront her with an illegitimate child.' His mouth twisted into an odd kind of smile. 'It seems that he is capable of respect, if not fidelity.'

'Is he…going to make you his heir?'

'He said something rather strange about that,' answered Xavier, recalling the way the Sheikh had brought it into the conversation almost absently—like a man reciting from a poem. 'That a crown could never be chosen, only inherited.'

'What does *that* mean?'

Xavier's eyes narrowed. He had already told her far too much—and now it seemed that she was getting turned on by the fact that one day he might rule a country like this. Would that make her more accessible to his bed? he wondered. Wasn't it about time he found out?

A pulse beat deep in his groin. Was he going crazy? Alone in a darkened room with a beautiful woman and what was he doing? *Telling* her stuff. Giving her access to his innermost thoughts. Instead of losing himself in the sweet sanctuary of her body.

He could feel the pulsing of his blood intensify as he stared at her. 'You have let your hair down,' he said suddenly.

Laura felt something in the atmosphere shift, alter. Something in his eyes had changed, too. Their blackness now seemed a beguiling contradiction—like a kaleidoscope which could change from moment to moment, from hard and glittering to soft with promise.

'You have let your hair down,' he repeated huskily. 'Running like a blood-red waterfall down your back.'

It was an erotic image and her mouth dried to dust, all her earlier fluency dissolved by the sensual caress of his words.

Slowly and deliberately he hooked a finger in the air to beckon to her.

'*Viens*,' he whispered. 'Come here.'

It should have been easy to say no—and if he had said the same thing earlier, in a different mood and at a different time, then Laura might have done.

But his disclosures had changed something—had smashed through her defences to leave her vulnerable to the longing which was now flooding into her unguarded body. He had reached out to her in a way she could never have imagined, and his confidences had humbled her and made her feel connected to him in a way that somehow went beyond the physical attraction she had felt for him from the word go. She wanted more than sex from this black-eyed Frenchman. She wanted to hold him and to comfort him, to draw him to her breast and stroke his ruffled black hair—but did she dare? Did she dare give in to those desires?

He raised his eyebrows. Had he ever had to ask a woman more than once? Never! 'Yet you hesitate?'

Laura drank in his dark beauty while a fierce battle raged within her. Would it be so wrong? He had paved the way for intimacy with all the things he had just told her—surely that must mean he also respected her?

And wouldn't this be a kind of balm to her spirit—to help erase the memories of her disastrous time with Josh with a man who seemed to be everything a woman could ever want?

And then what? What if you give your heart to him—

because this man is in a different league from Josh, and he could easily smash it into a million pieces?

She wouldn't.

Men could just enjoy sex for what it was—so why couldn't a woman? Lots of her friends did.

And, silencing the doubts which began to bubble to the surface of her mind, Laura gave in to her heart's desire. She stood up and walked straight into his waiting arms.

CHAPTER EIGHT

UNSEEN in the half-light, Xavier's lips curved into a hard smile—his desire briefly dominated by triumph as he took Laura's soft body into his arms. Yet even as he thrilled at the very touch of her was he not aware of a faint trace of disappointment?

It had been as easy as it always was! Ah, if only she knew how much her uncertainty had turned him on—how the short wait had tantalised him—then might not she have made him wait a little longer?

His thumb skated down over her peaking breast and he felt her shudder. 'Do you know how long I have wanted to touch your breasts like this?' he questioned idily.

Laura closed her eyes with pleasure. 'No.'

'Well, you should. From the moment you walked into my office I wanted to take your clothes off.'

'Do you...do you think like that about all women?' she asked shakily, aware that this line of questioning might take her into dangerous waters.

'All women? *Non.* But a woman as beautiful as you—ah, *oui*—then it is certain!'

Laura stiffened. *So don't ask him stuff if you can't bear to hear the answer!*

'Relax, *cherie*,' he urged softly. 'Don't think about the others—for it is you who are here with me now.' And then he bent his head close to her ear, so that she could feel his breath warm on her neck. 'Do you know that I could continue to touch you like this until the end of time? Do you?'

Tracing a soft line over her nipple, his thumb circled a featherlight path of pleasure so intense that it was easy to let the troublesome thoughts just slip away. Laura closed her eyes in a delirious mixture of shock and pleasure. This was supposed to be just sex, so why did it feel like getting on a fast train to paradise? *Already!*

'Xavier,' she breathed in disbelief.

He moved his hand to cup the other. How completely she capitulated. And what a contradiction—the buttoned-up lawyer with the soft siren beneath. He bent his head to brush his lips against the sensitised mound, his tongue teasing her nipple so that his voice was muffled. 'I could take it into my mouth and lick you there until you cried out your pleasure. Has a man ever made you come from sucking your breast alone, *cherie*?'

Something in the erotic boast unnerved her—despite Laura's vow to just enjoy this for what it was without reading anything else into it. Xavier must have known some of the greatest lovers in the world—so how could she possibly compete?

'Have they?' he prompted silkily.

Suddenly, she was scared. The man whose dark head was bent over her breast was intent on pleasure but what if she couldn't pleasure him back? What if he thought she was some racy, experienced type? How would he react when he discovered the truth of her relative inexperience?

'Kiss me, Xavier,' she whispered nervously, as she clutched his shoulders with her trembling hands. 'Just kiss me!'

Her unsophisicated little plea startled him, and he straightened up to look down into her face, lifting her chin with the tip of his finger. Her green eyes were like two huge, glittering emeralds in her pale, heart-shaped face, with her glorious red hair tumbling free.

How wild and beautiful she looked, he thought, as he drove his mouth hungrily down on hers. But something in the breathless wonder of that first touch affected him, and the kiss became something other than what he had been expecting. Hard and hungry became soft and caressing, and then a sweet melding, and then—like the most glorious intimacy—the meeting and exploration of two mouths.

On and on the kiss went, as her arms reached up to entwine themselves around him like delicate vines, and Xavier felt weak with the intensity of it—forcing himself to concentrate on the hot, urgent shaft of his erection. But he felt he was fighting on so many fronts. His startling paternity. The way she made him feel. Himself.

'Laura,' he groaned.

He spoke the word into her open mouth and Laura trembled. 'What is it?' she whispered.

He wanted to say *Don't kiss me like that.* He wanted her to act dirty—*that* was how he liked his women to behave in the bedroom. Not like…like…

With ruthless erotic efficiency he began to stroke her. 'How can I play with you when you make me want to rip this exquisite nightgown from your body, push you up against the wall and take you like I was a teenage boy?' he demanded unsteadily. 'Tell me, is that how you like it? Hot and fast? Or slow and sweet?'

'I don't know,' she whispered, wondering what a man of the world would like best.

At another time and in another place her submissive reply might have been one of the most erotic things anyone had ever said to him. But coming on top of the emotional impact of the evening and his subsequent unburdening to her, Xavier felt exposed—as if the dry, gritty sand of the desert was being buffeted against his naked body.

'You don't know?' he repeated sarcastically.

She was going to mess up; she knew it. Josh had been right. 'Show me.'

Show her? He tensed as the unbelievable flew into his head. *'Mon Dieu,'* he breathed. 'You're not a virgin?'

Was that how she appeared—as fumbling and inexperienced as if she had no knowledge of men? 'Of course not.'

What the hell was he thinking of—asking a question which risked making a fool of him? Since he had been transported to this exotic and unknown land he had started inventing fairytales—was that it? As if a woman of her age who looked like she did would be a virgin!

Oh, yes—he would show her, all right. He began to slide the slippery silk up her leg, splaying his hands and stroking his fingertips along the soft surface of her inner thigh until she gasped.

'Unbutton my shirt,' he instructed unevenly.

Laura complied, silently willing her fingers not to fumble, but she was so eaten up with nerves and excitement that it wasn't easy. Please make this everything I think it could be and want it to be. Or was that asking too much? 'My hands are trembling,' she admitted.

'So I see,' he said drily.

'Xavier!' she gasped, just as his mouth dipped to kiss the curve between neck and shoulder, just as his hand slipped down between her legs to where the heat was most intense.

'Shall I make you come first with my finger?' he mused. 'And then my tongue? And then with…this?'

He guided her hand down to where he was exquisitely hard. Just let go, she told herself. If this is the only night you have with him, then why not give in to your every fantasy? 'No,' she whispered as she touched the rocky ridge of him. 'I want to feel you inside me.'

'*Mon Dieu!*' he moaned. 'You drive me crazy! You touch me and you talk to me like…' Like what? Not like a virgin, no. But with some quality which made it feel special, different. As if she was speaking from the heart.

He was used to worldly lovers who used polished and erotic skills to *pleasure* him—but there was something so *unaffected* about the way Laura reacted to him. As if it really *mattered*. Xavier tensed. And it didn't matter.

Who cared if she was unworldly? She was a woman he had been foolish enough to confide in—but that was done now, and this was the perfect opportunity to wipe that memory away and replace it with something else.

In that second, something in Xavier's resolve changed, and he felt it in the almost imperceptible hardening of his body. It was time to demonstrate his finesse, to make love to her in such a way that every man who followed would provide just a pale imitation of the pleasure she had known with him.

Without warning, he lifted her up into his arms.

'What are you doing?'

'What do you think? I am taking you to bed because I want to enjoy you in comfort,' he ground out, as he began to carry her towards his bedroom.

Enjoy you in comfort.

She couldn't work out whether that was sexy or insulting. But her craven body told her that it was too late to back out now, and she just leaned back against his hard chest as he carried her into his bedroom.

Her first thought was that this room was on a much

more lavish scale than hers, but then he was laying her down on the bed and towering over her like a dark statue—his black eyes gleaming as they swept over her in sensual assessment.

'I think that I am wearing a little too much, don't you?' he observed, as he peeled his shirt off and tossed it aside.

Laura swallowed. His torso was rock-hard and honed with muscle, and the sprinkling of dark hair on his chest arrowed enticingly down to where he began to unbuckle his belt.

He saw her emerald eyes widen as he began to slide the zip down, and he smiled, because this was how he liked it.

This was Xavier in control. Xavier about to pleasure a woman and then walk away, as he always did. Maybe not today, or even tomorrow—but walk he would eventually, without a backward glance or a single doubt.

'Xavier,' Laura whispered, because as he slid his trousers off she became suddenly daunted by the sheer magnificence of his body. Those tensile thighs, like iron itself, and narrow hips, and…Laura closed her eyes.

'Open your eyes,' he said softly, as he moved onto the bed and pulled her into his arms, a frown creasing his brow. 'Why do you shiver so? You are frightened? Because I am so big?'

'Daunted.'

He gave a cool laugh. 'You have the lawyer's precision with words—but this is no time for them, and you are wearing far too many clothes. *Viens ici.*'

He slid her negligee off, and the matching night-gown—until she was as naked as he was. He groaned as he looked at the lush breasts and the enticing triangle of dark red hair between her thighs.

'Later I shall feast my eyes on you,' he murmured. 'But first we shall feast on each other, because my hunger is too great to wait any longer.' Xavier bent his dark head to take the puckered rosy tip of her nipple into his mouth, his tongue flicking around it, his teeth gently grazing.

A shaft of desire shot through her. 'Oh!' gasped Laura, her head falling back against the pillow. 'Oh, Xavier!'

Xavier lifted his head and murmured his appreciation as the dark red hair tumbled into a fiery waterfall down her back. He let his tongue move between her breasts, roving to the dip of her navel, then continuing on an inexorable path downwards. Laura caught hold of his shoulders.

'No!' she cried. 'Xavier, please.'

He heard the raw appeal in her voice and something touched him through the slow burn of desire. He lifted his head again, ebony eyes narrowed. 'You don't like that?'

She wasn't really sure, because Josh had never been a big fan—and it suddenly seemed just too matter-of-fact to discuss their erotic preferences like this. Like going shopping in some sort of sexual supermarket, and she didn't want it to be like that.

Laura had convinced herself that this was never going to be anything more than great sex—but she was only human, and wasn't there also the very romantic side which no woman could ever quite suppress? That dreamed of hearts and flowers and happy-ever-after when she was intimate with a man? And even if they didn't mean it, *then* surely they could *pretend*?

'What is it that you want, *cherie*?' he questioned, sensing her doubts.

'I want you. Properly.' She didn't want him to perform a million of his clever little variations on a theme, for she was terrified that she wouldn't know how to respond to half of them, terrified that he might compare her to other women he had known who did.

'Tell me,' he murmured, and put his face very close to hers.

'I want you to fill me. I want…I want…'

'Want what, Little Miss Lawyer?' he teased, even though he was aching in a way he had never ached before. 'Don't tell me that a word has escaped you.'

'I want to feel you,' she said boldly. 'Inside me.'

Xavier could not see her blush, but he could feel it in the warmth of her cheek against his, and suddenly he felt more than a little overwhelmed. Was it because a blush was something a woman couldn't fake? Because it was a true glimpse into the way she was feeling—and Laura was feeling *shy* about making a request that had sounded so *delightful* to his ears.

'Then feel me you will,' he said starkly. 'Right… *now*.'

He moved over her, bending his head to kiss her as he thrust into her and set about making love to her as if it was a masterclass. He loved to take women to the edge over and over again, until they were begging him to put an end to their sweet torment. But Laura was different.

She kissed him a lot. She touched his face a lot. She ruffled his hair with her fingers and traced light little patterns across his skin with her fingertips until he shuddered—and he couldn't work out why. But she made love as if it was important—and even though it wasn't it didn't seem to affect his response to her.

So that for once it was Xavier who was lost—swept away on a wave of something so...so delicious that it defied description.

Afterwards he lay looking up at the moon-dappled ceiling, telling himself that it was just an incredible orgasm. But Laura's head was leaning against the crook of his arm and her hair was spread all over his chest, and he fell asleep with a much deeper feeling of contentment than usual.

CHAPTER NINE

MOLTEN gold morning sun flooded over her bare skin and Laura blinked as her eyes accustomed themselves to the light. Someone must have opened the shutters. She yawned, still disorientated in the aftermath of a fitful night spent…

Her eyes snapped open as she turned her head to see the empty rumpled space beside her.

A night spent making love with Xavier de Maistre!

'Good morning,' came a soft voice from the other side of the room. And there was Xavier. He was naked, except for a tiny towel wrapped around his hips, and his hair was still damp from the shower. And he was watching her as a wary biologist might observe a newly discovered species.

'Did you sleep well?'

'I…' She met his eyes. He had woken her three times in the night to make love to her. It had been the best night of her life, and at one point she thought she might have told him so. Had he forgotten all that—or did things you said while you were having sex simply not count? Was this the language of sophisticated lovers—that next morning you acted as if nothing had happened? Or was he using a subtle code to warn her not to make it into something it wasn't—not to come out with gushing words of praise for his undeniable sexual prowess or—worse—to tell him how easy it would be to fall in love with him?

Well, she would take her cue from him. They were both adults—she wasn't going to play coy or cringing or regretful or anything else negative. She had enjoyed every second of it—and so, presumably, had he.

'No, I feel great this morning,' she murmured back.

He walked over to the bed and kissed her hair. 'You smell great, too.'

'So…so do you.'

Their eyes met as he slipped his hand between her legs, and suddenly Laura felt shy without the concealment of darkness and kind shadows cloaking expressions and hiding any tell-tale signs of vulnerability or insecurity.

'Xavier.'

'Mmm?'

'I think I ought to be getting up.'

'Shh, that's my job. Take the towel off,' he instructed on a sultry whisper.

Had she thought she needed darkness to feel liberated? Well, that just went to prove how wrong she could be—because with him touching her in that light, teasing way Laura was suddenly overwhelmed with desire, and she pulled the towel from him and tossed it away.

'Like that?'

'*D'accord.* Just like that!' He shuddered and closed his eyes as she encircled him. 'Mmm—that is so good, *cherie.*'

'Is it?' Made bold by his murmured praise, Laura rubbed her hand up and down him in a wanton way which seemed both alien to her and yet utterly right. Or was that just the Xavier effect? Making a relatively inexperienced woman suddenly feel as if she would like to work her way through the entire *Kama Sutra*? 'How good?'

'Too good,' he groaned, and, snatching her hand away, lifted her up and slowly lowered her onto him instead, placing his hands on either side of her hips and moving her up and down on his body, while he pierced her honeyed sweetness with his thick shaft. It was unbearably erotic to see the contrast of her pale skin with the thick curtain of dark red hair which spilled down over her rose-tipped breasts. But her eyes were closed. 'Look at me,' he urged. 'Laura, look at me.'

Laura did—feeling suddenly shy. For it seemed the most intimate act of all for their eyes to meet and hold while he thrust into her. She felt her pleasure suddenly escalating out of control—her heart contracting along with her body as a great whooshing wave of emotion began to carry her away.

'I can't wait,' she cried out as spasms of profound pleasure began to pull her under.

Xavier's felt her tighten around him. 'Then don't,' he urged, helpless himself when, minutes later, he let go and was sent shooting into orbit by another orgasm of such intensity that his heart seemed to stop for a brief moment. And when the waves of pleasure had died away he was shaken as that feeling stole over him again—the lazy contentment which made minutes drift into hours, so that he must have slept.

When he awoke it was to find Laura lying watching him—and as he stretched luxuriously he wondered if they could get away with spending the whole day in bed.

'Hello, again,' he said, and stretched lazily.

Laura knew she had to pull herself together. She had been lying there watching him while he was sleeping— the two thick black arcs of his lashes feathering the dark olive skin. Mainly, she'd been feeling a kind of dazed bliss.

In sleep he looked softer—almost vulnerable. Yet hadn't there been traces of that same vulnerability when he had been telling her about his reaction upon meeting the man who had sired him? Or was that just Laura projecting what Laura wanted to see?

'Hello,' she said, and then, employing her usual sharp thinking instead of some love-hungry little-girl yearning, she forced herself to confront the reality of the situation.

Fact: they had just had sex.

Fact: Xavier was here to spend time with his father, not to be in bed with his father's lawyer.

So what would any other woman do in this situation? She would give him a cool thanks-for-the-memory kind of smile and she would get out early, with her dignity and her pride and her heart still intact.

'I'd better go,' she whispered, and even managed to lean over to plant a kiss on his nose.

Xavier shook his head. 'Let's ring for coffee,' he yawned.

'I'd rather not—I don't want anyone to know I'm in bed with you.'

'Why not? Malik didn't make you sign a vow of celibacy before you arrived, did he?'

'Of course not,' said Laura. 'I just don't particularly want to broadcast what we've been doing, if it's all the same with you.'

'Oh, come on.' He gave a slow, cynical smile. 'You would have to be *very* naïve if you believed that anything which goes on within the walls of this Palace isn't already known by Malik and his spies.' He tilted her chin with his finger. 'And I am sure that this bewitching lawyer is far from naïve.'

There was something in his tone she didn't like—something which was making her regret what had happened.

Determined not to make a big deal of it, Laura slid off the bed and began to pull on her clothes as unselfconsciously as possible—which wasn't easy with those eyes following her every move.

It wasn't until she had dressed and composed her face into the kind of even-though-we've-just-had-sex-I'm-not-going-to-come-over-all-heavy-on-you expression she knew was expected, that she dared to look at him again. And despaired that her heart melted at just the sight of him.

'So what are you going to do now?' she asked.

She had clammed up, he thought suddenly. Retreated from him in a way he was unused to. His eyes narrowed. Now, why was that? 'I presume you aren't talking breakfast?'

'No.' Her cool expression was starting to slip, and Laura was torn between wanting to be spirited out of there and wanting to climb back into bed and into his arms. 'I meant how long are you planning to stay here, in Kharastan?'

Xavier stretched his arms above his head, not bothering to hide his nakedness or the fact that watching her slipping on her underwear had been enough to make his body stir once more. He ached. He wanted her again— but he was damned if he was going to beg her to get back into bed with him. Women did not usually leave his bed unless he asked or ordered them to. *He* was the one who left it first!

Frustration bubbled over into anger, but he sublimated it with a cool look.

'Are you interested from a professional or a personal point of view?' he questioned.

Laura's heart missed a beat. There was something in his voice she didn't like. Was he worried that she was going to start getting all clingy and possessive? And warning her not to?

'Professional, of course,' she said crisply.

'I haven't decided what I'm going to do yet,' he said slowly.

His troubled face in the dead of the night came back to haunt her. It had torn at her heart then and it tore at it now. 'Why not stay?' asked Laura gently. Because— no matter what the outcome of their intimacy—she felt that he owed it to himself to explore his roots. 'And get to know your father.'

'You think I should?'

Did that mean he valued her opinion? Laura felt as if she'd been given some kind of moral reprieve and nodded her head. 'Definitely!'

Xavier's black eyes narrowed suspiciously as everything suddenly began to click into place. How completely she had switched from cool to passionate, then back to cool again. Her seemingly inexplicable appearance in his room last night, wearing clothes designed to seduce—as indeed all her clothes were.

During the journey from the Sheikh's apartments back to his room, had Malik somehow got word to her that Xavier's mood was dark and unpredictable? Had she been told to pacify him in the most elemental way known to women?

'How very persuasive you are, *cherie*,' he murmured. 'Tell me, is that also part of your brief—to convince me to stay?'

Something in his tone sent another whisper of alarm along her spine and the meaning behind his question became clear. Laura stared into eyes suddenly grown cold and thought how little she really knew of him. How could you connect with a man on a physical level, which at moments last night had seemed almost spiritual, and yet when you came back down to earth all that was left was emptiness and suspicion?

'I told you,' she said stiffly. 'My job was simply to bring you here.'

'And sleeping with me?' he drawled. 'Would you define that as a perk—or a condition?'

Laura froze, for a moment thinking that he couldn't possibly have meant it. But one look at the icy set of his features told her that he had. 'If I were the hysterical type I might just slap your face for that remark—but as I'm not I'll treat it with the contempt it deserves.'

'But you enjoyed it,' he challenged softly. 'In fact I'd go so far as to say you absolutely *loved* it—so I'd say it definitely fell into the category of perk, wouldn't you?'

Something about the way he said it reminded Laura of how eagerly she had writhed beneath him. The way she had wrapped her thighs around his back and the way her body had arched ecstatically beneath his. How she would have loved to tell him no—that as a lover he was a dead loss—that she had endured what had happened with gritted teeth. But he knew and she knew that would be the biggest lie of all.

'Oh, you're right. I did love it—the sex was great,' she said. 'But then I expect it always is—men don't get reputations as super-lovers without it being backed up by fact.'

'Why, thank you, *cherie*,' he drawled.

'It wasn't supposed to be a compliment!' she snapped. 'If you want to know, I think that going around seducing everything that moves is a pretty sad and empty way to live.'

'Whereas dressing to seduce and luring men back for wealthy Middle-Eastern potentates *isn't* sad and empty, I suppose?' he snapped.

Laura opened her mouth to tell him that the silk-satin clothes she wore were a million miles away from the way she usually dressed—but surely to do that would only bring substance to his argument? If she admitted that her wardrobe had been commissioned by the Palace—and at great cost—he might reasonably ask why her clothes had been of such importance. And, in a way, she wasn't completely blameless, was she? When she had been told to acquire the expensive garments she had readily agreed, hadn't she?

Because she had wanted the job, that was why—and because she had been willing to play the part she had been complicit in their schemes. But if she had allowed herself to be decorated like a cake—then she couldn't really complain if Xavier had wanted to take a slice of her for himself, could she?

Because you didn't have to let him!

She lifted her chin, telling herself that his last memory of her would be as a strong, proud woman, and not one who was crumbling inside and wishing it could be different.

'You know what?' she said. 'A constant stream of different women throughout your life means that you can cleverly avoid any intimacy and commitment, and that's okay—that's your choice. There will always be willing and available women for a man like you, Xavier.' She leaned forward, banishing self-interest and regret from her agenda, her green eyes on fire. 'But you've only got one father—remember that—though maybe the one you *have* got doesn't fit in with your particular image.'

Xavier stared at her. 'What are you talking about?'

'Maybe it will suit you to have a rich father you never knew. Maybe it makes you feel better—knowing you were denied access and forced to spend your early life in poverty. Though, ironically, that's probably the main factor in your success.' She studied him as dispassionately as was possible. 'Maybe you're one of those people who likes going through life with a reason to be angry—thinking it makes their unreasonable behaviour in some way acceptable. Well, it doesn't—not in my book.'

'How dare you speak to me like this?'

'Isn't it time that someone had the courage to?'

'Get out!' he flared furiously.

Laura suddenly felt the most delicious and heady sensation of power. 'I think you're forgetting yourself, Xavier. I don't work for *you* and therefore I don't take orders from you—and besides, I was leaving anyway, remember? I've got some paperwork to do, and after that I'm going to ask Malik to get me on the next flight out of here!'

Feeling his eyes burning into her back, Laura stalked out. It was possibly the most stylish exit she had ever made, but the satisfaction of knowing that did nothing to hide the pain she felt inside.

CHAPTER TEN

'DO YOU have *any* idea how much longer Malik will be?' questioned Laura, trying like mad to hold onto her temper, which was becoming more frayed by the second.

'You will be informed just as soon as he becomes available,' said his secretary smoothly, and Laura stared mutinously at his back as he disappeared through the door of Malik's office.

She had been kept waiting outside the office of the Sheikh's aide for almost forty minutes—growing angrier by the minute. She couldn't even go back to her suite—because Xavier was there and, having stormed out of his bedroom, she would look and feel a fool if she had to go crawling back again.

Yet neither could she just pack her bags and leave. She had flown here by private jet, she was the Sheikh's special guest, and as such it was going to be difficult to make her own travel arrangements and get back again. She wasn't even sure if there *were* any scheduled flights back to the UK—they almost certainly wouldn't be direct.

And they were bound to be expensive. Having gone to all this trouble earn herself enough money to get herself out of a financial fix, wouldn't it be a bit stupid if she then blew a large chunk of it on a ticket because her pride had been hurt and she felt used?

The sensible thing to do would be to wait and speak to Malik and gently remind him—if it came to it—that he was contractually obliged to pay her and send her home.

The door to Malik's large suite of offices opened and another of the male secretaries appeared, and bowed.

'Miss Cottingham,' he said, in the now familiar Kharastani accent. 'Malik Al-Ahal asks that you meet with him in the Perfumed Garden—will you please follow me?'

Laura frowned. Had Malik exited from his offices by a different entrance, or had she been misled into thinking that he had been there all along? Not that she would bother asking his secretary, she thought, as she stepped out into the brilliant Kharastan day. His undoubted loyalty to his boss told her it would be a waste of time.

Instead, Laura forced herself to concentrate on the beauty of the Palace gardens and try to erase the beauty of Xavier's face and body from her mind. Because a man could not be said to be beautiful or handsome— not if he had a black soul and a suspicious mind, and would pluck a woman up as if she were a flower to then be crushed underfoot.

But he could only do that if a woman let him.

The torment of her thoughts was momentarily

soothed by the sweet scent of the flowers which drifted out from the Perfumed Garden. It was intoxicating and evocative, and Laura breathed in deeply as she followed the secretary through an arched arbour, where honeysuckle grew in wild profusion.

And there was Malik—standing with his back to her as he snipped a perfect white rose from its bush.

He must have heard her footstep, for he turned when he heard her and said something rapidly in his native tongue to his secretary, who bowed deeply, then left.

Malik held the rose out towards her. 'You will accept this flower?'

Laura's face was grave. 'Only if I can be certain it comes without obligation.'

Malik raised his eyebrows. 'Perhaps you will tell me why you insisted on this meeting?'

'Because I want to finish up whatever work is left and go home—to England.'

'I'm afraid that may not be possible.'

Laura's blood ran cold. It was worse than her worst fantasies. 'What do you mean—not possible? My boss knows I'm out here, and he'll get worried if he doesn't hear—he's expecting me back at work,' she breathed. 'So you can't keep me here against my will!'

Malik gave a short laugh. 'My dear Miss Cottingham! We do much trade with England, and I do not think that the government of your country would look kindly on us if we started keeping its young women prisoners!'

Laura stared at him suspiciously. 'Then why won't you let me go home?'

'It might be a little more…' Malik hesitated '…*convenient* if you stayed. Just for a couple more days, you understand?'

But it was a velvet-cloaked order, not a polite request, and realisation slowly began to dawn on her. 'This is Xavier's doing, isn't it? He has demanded this?'

Malik didn't react.

'*Isn't* it?' questioned Laura.

Malik shrugged. 'You cannot blame the man for wanting you to remain here as his…companion—not in view of what has happened.'

Did Laura imagine the faint note of censure in his voice, or was she just feeling vulnerable and raw? 'I'm not with you,' she said. But then she saw the way he lowered his eyes, and suddenly she knew exactly what he meant.

He *did* know that she'd slept with Xavier—had Xavier told him, or had one of the servants gossiped? Laura was aware of the sting of colour to her cheeks, knowing that to try to defend herself would be a doomed enterprise certain to lead to even more embarrassment.

What excuse or reason could she give to condone her behaviour in a country where a woman's honour was as highly prized as rubies? She could not even offer up deep emotion as a contributing factor—who would believe her when she had known Xavier for such a short time?

Yet it was not as it must have looked to an outsider. Deep emotion *had* been there—well, certainly on

Laura's part. She had wanted to comfort him as well as to be made love to. She had wanted to touch him in ways which were more than physical—the sad thing was that she had ever believed she *could*. Something strong and powerful had reached out to her—something so rare that she had felt nothing remotely like it in all her twenty-six years.

But now?

Laura bit her lip, wondering if she had been completely stupid. Whether what had happened had been all about her writing the script for what she *wanted* it to be—rather than the reality of what it was.

But if Xavier thought that she was going to continue with the intimacy, then he was badly mistaken. What was done was done—she couldn't blame him for taking what she had so freely offered—but now it was time to look after herself.

'This is intolerable, Malik,' she said in a low voice, but the Kharastani man was shaking his head.

'Only if you make it so,' he demurred.

'But we have interconnecting rooms,' she pointed out.

'And you have a key,' he said sharply.

He didn't say *And maybe you should have used it before*—but he didn't have to. It was all there, written on his face, and Laura flinched.

'And I suppose that if I make a fuss then my salary will suffer? You'll withhold it—or use complicated international machinery to delay payment for so long that by the time I get it I'll no longer need it?' she challenged.

Malik's eyes widened fractionally, as if matters as vulgar as money were not talked about within the rarefied surroundings of the Palace, but Laura didn't care. She was not—like him—cushioned by the untold wealth of a royal family and its courtiers. She was a working girl.

'I must ensure that everyone is kept happy,' he said.

'Everyone except me, that is,' returned Laura as she recognised her predicament. She had no choice other than to stay, but at least she could word it to sound as if it had been *her* decision—her wounded pride demanded that much. 'Well, I'll stay for as long as it is necessary, but no longer. I'm not prepared to sacrifice my livelihood simply because I made a poor personal judgement.'

'I think it will not be as bad as you anticipate. For all its antiquity the Blue Palace has many facilities for you to enjoy,' countered Malik. 'There is an Olympic-sized pool, a gym—and our cinema houses the most up-to-the-minute films. And I have assigned Sidonia to cater for your every need.'

Laura raised her eyebrows. 'A gilded cage, you mean?'

'There are many ways of looking at a situation,' he said softly. 'You could always try to enjoy it.'

Laura met his eyes. 'If you say so.' But it wasn't as easy as that. If Xavier hadn't been part of the deal, then it might have been—but how could she enjoy what sounded like a state-of-the-art holiday camp if she was worrying about fighting him off? Or, worse, fighting off her own attraction to him?

She turned on her heel, not knowing or caring

whether she was supposed to wait for the Kharastani nobleman to leave first. If they were breaking the rules of her employment then she would damned well break a few of her own in return!

Emerging from the direction of the palace, Laura saw Sidonia walking towards her, and suddenly she was pleased to see the friendly and welcoming face of the servant.

'Good morning, Sidonia,' she said.

'Good morning.' Sidonia folded her hands together, the tips of her fingers beneath her chin, and gave the elegant bow of the traditional Kharistani greeting. 'You wish perhaps to take breakfast now?'

Laura shook her head. 'Not just yet. What I would really like is some exercise. Is there any way you could get hold of a swimsuit for me?'

Sidonia nodded, then spoke in her sweetly accented English. 'But of course. The pool is equipped with everything you could possibly require.'

'Just for me?' Laura wondered aloud as they walked towards the complex.

'For all our guests. The Sheikh often has visiting dignitaries who expect things to be primitive—it gives him great pleasure to show them how much a part of the modern world we are here at the Palace.'

Laura shot the servant a curious look as they walked past exquisite flowerbeds, each symmetrically planted with a different colour theme—scarlets, golds and blues. Her pride in her Palace and her Ruler were touching.

'From the air, the flowers in this part of the garden resemble our Kharastan flag,' said Sidonia. 'You see the shape of the falcon's head?'

'Yes, I do.' Laura smiled. 'Your English is so good.'

Sidonia nodded. 'I am pleased with my progress—but the credit for that must go to Sorrel.'

The name rang a bell, and Laura remembered the young blonde woman who had appeared at the banquet, summoning Xavier to the Sheikh, and nodded. 'Is that Malik's ward?' she questioned, and Sidonia nodded. 'How did that happen?'

'Her parents were the British representatives here in Kharastan—both great Middle Eastern scholars,' said Sidonia. 'They died in an aircrash over the mountains of Maraban and everyone thought that Sorrel would go straight home. But she had grown up here and loved it—she considered Kharastan to be her home and was reluctant to leave. She attended the university here—very few English women are fluent in the Kharastan language. One day she will go back to England, but she will not do so until the Sheikh dies.'

Laura wondered how much Sorrel—and indeed Sidonia—knew about Xavier. Were they aware that he was the Sheikh's son—perhaps with a legitimate claim on his kingdom? And what if Xavier made no claim, or did not meet with the Sheikh's approval? Who would rule Kharastan then?

For some reason Malik's face swam into Laura's mind, but they had reached the poolhouses now, and she was dazzled by the sheer opulent splendour of the pool. It was a vast rectangle of perfectly clear water, and it was lined with beautiful golden and blue mosaics which depicted scenes of Kharastan life. The poolhouses themselves were the very last word in luxury—with a steamroom and sauna making it look like a lavish and very exclusive health club.

'You will find everything you need here,' said Sidonia.

'Thank you,' said Laura, as she gazed round in delight. 'And I wonder if you could bring me some day clothes from my room? Perhaps trousers might be suitable?'

'Certainly.'

After Sidonia had gone, Laura selected a plain black costume and dived into the water, emerging like a seal mid-way down the pool and beginning to swim. She had been good at swimming as a child—with free baths close to their home. Often—if her mother had been working in the evenings—Laura would go there straight from school, swimming length after length in a steady crawl.

It had always invigorated her rather than tired her out, and it did the same now—so that by time she had finished her swim she felt ready to face anything.

Afterwards, Laura showered and changed into the linen trousers and silk shirt Sidonia had brought—tying her damp hair back with a green ribbon which echoed the colour of the jade and silver beads she slung round her neck. Narrow sandals were slipped onto her bare feet and she felt in control.

She looked just right—cool, sophisticated and sleek.

Now Laura could see that the Sheikh's insistence that she wear designer clothes from top to toe had been about much more than dressing to lure Xavier back here—as he had accused her. It meant that she didn't look out of place in these august surroundings. That she looked as if she fitted in. And that was rather a nice feeling.

'I'd like breakfast now, Sidonia. Is it possible to eat outside?' she asked the maidservant.

'But of course!'

A table was set for her beneath the dappled canopy of some exotic large-leafed tree, and she was just spooning mulberry jam onto her plate when a shadow fell over her. She looked up, her heart beginning to pound in her chest when she saw who it was.

'Xavier!'

She was the first woman who had ever run from him, and yet here she was—looking cool and amazing in linen and silk, with the sun shining on her glossy red hair and some stunning beads emphasising the intense emerald of her eyes.

'You are hiding from me?' he asked silkily.

'Does it look like it? Hiding would imply fear, and even though it seems I am virtually a prisoner here the last thing I am is frightened!' she returned. 'Especially of you!'

Xavier smiled. Her feisty form was like a breath of fresh air after the tumult of the previous night. His meeting with the Sheikh had affected him more than he had anticipated. He had thought that sex with Laura would wipe it all away—his troubled feelings as well as his lust for her—but he had felt none of the expected sense of closure this morning.

So he had come looking for Laura, expecting... what? To find her tearstained or regretful—not sitting in the sunshine eating her breakfast!

'Then why did you run away?' he probed.

'Because your remarks to me were insulting.'

'So you weren't asked to seduce me to entice me to stay?' In the bright, clear air of the morning the accusation sounded ridiculous as soon as it fell from his lips.

'I'm a lawyer, Xavier—not a professional siren! Tell me, are the women you usually deal with unscrupulous enough to do something like that?'

He shrugged. 'Sometimes.'

'Then you've been mixing with the wrong kind of woman.'

Their eyes met in a long moment. 'Maybe I have,' he said slowly.

Laura saw the cat-like dilation of his black eyes and felt the tiptoe of awareness shivering its way down her spine. 'And that wasn't supposed to be a come-on!'

'Maybe I want it to be.'

But Laura shook her head, praying for the strength and resolve she needed. 'No, Xavier. And it's no good looking at me like that—I mean it.'

'No?' he echoed, in disbelief.

His arrogance was staggering! He thought he could say whatever he wanted to her and she would just lie back and let him make love to her!

'You are something else,' she breathed. 'But—just so that there's no misunderstanding—let me make myself clear. Sex with you was utterly fantastic, as I'm sure you know—but sex for women, *most* women, involves a lot more than that. Respect and self-worth play a pretty important part in the equation. If you really think me capable of going around and sleeping with different men on the Sheikh's say-so then you have only yourself to blame when I insist on keeping you at arm's length— no matter how good a lover you are.'

'You cannot mean this, Laura,' he objected. 'You have voiced your anger towards me, and I accept it. Perhaps I even deserved it. I apologise for the things I said to you. I take them back.' A smile curved the edges of his lips. 'There.'

Shaking her head, she pushed her chair back and stood up. 'You just don't get it, do you, Xavier? It can't just be made better with a grudging apology accompanied by a sexy smile.'

He could smell her newly washed hair and the faint drift of scent on her skin, and something about its innocent freshness made him want to groan aloud with frustration. 'But I want you, Laura—I want you *now*!'

'Read my lips,' she said, savouring the heady sensation of having taken back control. 'Which part of the word no don't you understand? There will be no intimacy. But that doesn't mean we can't be friends.'

'*Friends?*'

'There's no need to make it sound as if I've suggested something obscene—you do *have* friends, I suppose, Xavier?'

Of course he had friends—but no real close women-friends. And never lovers who *became* friends, because they always wanted to continue the intimate side of their relationship. And would Laura be any different, despite her vowed intentions?

Xavier's face was like stone, but beneath its unmoving exterior he felt the heavy pulsing of his blood as he stared down at her parted lips and her determined expression. The light of battle suddenly flared in his eyes.

No intimacy?

Like hell there wouldn't be!

CHAPTER ELEVEN

'YOUR resolve is admirably strong,' breathed Xavier in reluctant admiration. 'But I think that the strain of resisting what you really want is beginning to get to you—don't you, Laura? Your face is pale, despite the sun, and see how you tremble whenever I am near. And you really shouldn't lose any more weight—your body is quite perfect as it is.'

Never had Laura been so glad of the canopy of her wide-brimmed hat—which not only protected her pale skin from the scorching heat of the desert sun but also hid her face from Xavier's piercing black stare. Because if he had the opportunity to look closely he would discover that he was right—she *was* finding it difficult to withstand his relentless, sexy appeal.

Since their—she supposed you might call it showdown, they had spent nine days and nights in close confines within the walls of the Blue Palace, where she had learnt a surprising yet uncomfortable fact.

Naïvely, Laura had supposed that women didn't feel

sexual frustration in the same way as men did. She had certainly never been afflicted by it before. Her split with Josh had had rather terrifying financial repercussions, but she'd been greatly relieved at no longer having to endure his acrobatic but ultimately unsatisfactory style of lovemaking.

But this was different.

Lying in bed at night—knowing that the magnificent olive-skinned body of Xavier de Maistre was lying naked on the other side of the door she now insisted on locking...well. It would be enough to make any woman ache, surely—especially if she'd already tasted his sensual skills?

She considered his accusation now, as she slid two fingers easily inside the waistband of her trousers— *had* she lost weight? 'Everyone loses weight in hot weather,' she defended.

'But not everyone watches the object of her desire with hungry eyes instead of giving in to that desire. How stubborn you are, Laura.'

But Laura was less stubborn than concerned that her clever plan might have completely backfired on her. She had kept Xavier at arm's length and told him she wanted to be friends without realising that friendship broke down barriers in the same way that sex did.

If you lived very closely with a man and he wasn't kissing you the chances were he would have to talk to you, and you to him. And, as two foreigners in a strange land, they'd had plenty to talk about.

Laura had already decided that it would be easier if they liked each other—what she hadn't realised was how *easy* it would be to like him. Nor had she expected the look of admiration in his black eyes when she stuck to her guns and would not be swayed by his occasional flirtatious comments. It was as if he had been waiting for *her* resolve to crumble, and when it hadn't he had been forced to look at the situation—and her—in a completely different way.

Gradually, his expression of wry frustration had become replaced with a growing *respect,* and that made Laura feel good. It gave her back her *self*-respect, which meant she relaxed, and the more she relaxed the more he did—and, *oh*, that made her feel vulnerable all over again!

In her attempt to protect herself she had made herself susceptible to his careless charm, which was almost as devastating as his kiss.

She wiped the glow of sweat from her face as they stood on the summit overlooking the wide, sweeping plain of Kharastan's flat and rolling desert. The stark and dramatic country was becoming a little more familiar to her day by day—since every day something different had been laid on for the benefit of the Sheikh's honoured guests.

They had been to visit the bustling bazaars in the capital of Kumush Ay, and had been mesmerised by the sights and sounds and wonderful smells and bright colours of the busy marketplace. They had been taken to the formal riding school and witnessed a magnificent display by a troop of Akhal-Teke horses. And this morning they had come to watch Malik and a group of other Kharastani noblemen engage in the ancient sport of falconry.

Laura stood a little way back as she watched, aware of Xavier's rapt air of concentration and the realisation that this was very much a male bonding thing.

'Today we still practise this noble art as a mark of respect to the survival of our forefathers in the desert,' said Malik, as a terrifying-looking bird with cruel eyes perched on his leather-covered arm.

Xavier had revelled in his stay in the country—aware that he and Laura were being shown a variety of Kharastan life and recognising how rich and diverse it was. But through all the banquets, the shows and the lavish displays, he had remained somewhat on the sidelines. A spectator rather than a participant—until today. Under this beating desert sun, in this harsh and unforgiving terrain, something had happened to him.

Xavier had been captivated by the powerful raptor as it flew low across the coarse desert. Bobbing and veering like a drunk teetering home late at night, it shot high into the air as the lure was thrown. It was primitive and elemental, and in a moment of clarity he could suddenly see the point of the sport. But it was more than that.

It was like the click of understanding when you reached fluency in a foreign language. For the first time he allowed himself to feel the connection between himself and his forebears, to acknowledge his birthright.

His ancestors must have stood on this hot and harsh terrain, he thought, as tiny grains of sand whispered against his skin. When survival in the desert was a daily battle and falconry was not an elegant sport but a means of obtaining food. And at that moment he seemed a long long way from his elegant Parisian apartments.

It seemed that he was not who he had thought he was—instead he had discovered a man who was almost a stranger to himself. And he knew in that moment that he had changed, and that he could never go back to being the person he had been before. How could he? He was half-Kharastani!

The thought shook him—and, just like his early ancestors must have done, he sought refuge from his troubled thoughts in the calm balm of a woman's soothing presence.

He turned to look at Laura, who was standing watching the display with a mixture of fear and fascination, and he recognised that it had been her determination to push him away which had allowed him to focus his mind and his thoughts, like an athlete preparing for a big race. The absence of sex had filled him with a new and inner sense of purpose and—yes—of identity. But now he ached for her in a way he could never remember aching for a woman before.

Now, in the bright desert light, he narrowed his eyes to see if he could see the dark blot on the horizon which would herald the return of the strong, graceful bird they called the Saker Falcon. The skies remained clear, but inside Xavier was still troubled.

He thought of the local name for the Saker—hurr, meaning noble, or free. Malik had told him about it when they had come from Zahir's room last night, after one of their regular evening meetings with the Sheikh.

'How is Zahir?' Laura asked, her soft voice breaking into his thoughts.

Xavier looked at her, a picture of loveliness in the wide-brimmed hat which shielded her fair skin from the fierce Kharastani sun. He wanted to pull the ribbon from her hair and shake it loose, lose himself in its thick, scented satin. To feel rather than think—about *anything*—and yet she seemed determined to torment him, one way or another.

'He's about the same.' He shrugged.

'So what do you and he talk about, night after night?'

'*Sacre bleu*, but you stretch my patience, *cherie*!' Xavier laughed in spite of himself, for at that moment they saw the Saker contrasted against the bright sky, and there was whoop of joy from all the men. He turned to Laura, his face animated and alive with pleasure at the ancient ritual he had just witnessed. 'You keep me at arm's length, Laura—and yet you pry into my soul!'

Laura shook her head. 'I don't mean to pry, Xavier,' she said truthfully. 'I just wonder if it's good for you to keep everything bottled up—not to talk about this huge thing in your life that has happened. Unless you discuss it with Malik, of course?'

Xavier shook his head. The Sheikh's aide seemed to

have a curiously ambivalent attitude towards him. At times they were at ease together, yet at others there was tension and once—just once—Xavier had looked up and been surprised to see a look almost of *jealousy* there. Did he resent another man's growing closeness with the Sheikh? he wondered. After years of being his sole and trusted aide?

'No, I don't talk to Malik,' he said flatly.

'Then why not talk to me?' asked Laura, as she climbed into the back of their four-wheel drive and Xavier got in beside her, before the car moved away in a cloud of desert dust.

'Why should I do that?'

'Well, I'm a good listener. I'm impartial—and I'm honest enough to tell you what I think rather than what you want to hear—which in your case is no bad thing.'

'Are you quite possibly perfect in every way?' he asked, in a voice which was silkily sardonic.

When they'd first arrived here Laura might have viewed this question as making fun of her. But she had altered—was altering—she could feel it happening even now. She had stood firm in her resolve not to be a compliant bedfellow that he would soon tire of, and had regained her self-respect by managing to resist his breathtaking allure.

Friendship you had to work harder at than sexual chemistry—but she felt they were getting there.

But it was much bigger than just what *she* had got out of the experience. Laura had been looking outwards,

as well as inwards. She could see the chase of conflicting emotions in Xavier's eyes, and suddenly found that
she wanted to help him come to terms with what was
happening to *him*.

'Quite possibly completely perfect,' she agreed, half
turning in her seat to look at him. 'Tell me if you want.
Don't if you don't.'

Her neck was like a graceful arc, down which the
rope of dark red hair fell like plaited silk. What did he
have to lose? 'In the absence of much more distracting
pursuits I can see no alternative to talking,' he said. 'Yet
are you bound by professional confidence, Laura—or
will you be contracting my story to the highest-bidding
journalist on our return to the West?'

She shook her head and sighed in mock despair. 'You
have such a low view of other people.'

'It is based on experience,' he observed. 'Women
selling stories about my prowess as a lover! Business
rivals describing me as unscrupulous.'

'You probably *are* a bit unscrupulous, though,
aren't you?'

He stared at her for a long moment, and then unex-
pectedly began to laugh. 'Ah, but you are outrageous,
cherie,' he murmured admiringly.

The compliment warmed her more than it should
have done—and Laura forced a prim smile. 'If you
don't want women to sell their story, you should get to
know them properly before you have sex with them!'

He slanted her a look. 'Like I did with you, you mean?'

Laura blushed. 'That was cheap.'

He nodded. 'Yes, it was,' he agreed—because what he had shared with Laura felt anything but cheap.

The colour began to fade from her cheeks. 'If you're worried about confidentiality—I would never break the confidence of a friend.'

Was it because of her job that he found himself wanting to talk to her? Yet he had dated lawyers before without feeling the need to bare his soul, hadn't he? *But you have never found yourself in a situation quite like this one.* And hadn't talking been the precursor to that incredible night he had spent with her?

He felt free with her. Free to be able to put his thoughts into words and not have them stored in an emotional bank to be used against him. It was like allowing yourself to swim naked in the sea after years of being restricted by a tight rubber wetsuit.

'It's weird,' he said thoughtfully. 'It's just the little things that make you realise. The Sheikh is left-handed, and so am I. He never watches television but he devours non-fiction, and so do I. He is shrunken now by age, but his eyes…'

He had seen a photo of the Sheikh in his glorious youth—strong and indominitable—taken long before he had met his mother. But seeing the man in the flesh, even shrivelled flesh, was profoundly different—for in that virile face Xavier had caught a glimpse of himself, a merging of past and present which was a whole new and slightly shattering experience.

'His eyes are the same as yours?' guessed Laura.

'Yes,' he said simply. 'Exactly the same.

Laura suspected that on one level Xavier knew that traits such as left-handedness and eye-colour were inherited—but some things went beyond mere science. It was the human connection which was the important one here—the missing link in his life which had now been joined up.

'Do you think this discovery will change how you live your life from now on?' she asked quietly.

It was a perfectly reasonable question, he supposed—and yet he reacted badly to it, like someone allergic to strawberries being exposed to the refreshment tent at Wimbledon.

'You are suggesting there is something wrong with the way in which I live my life?'

Laura shrugged.

'Aren't you?' he persisted softly. 'I want to know, Laura.'

What did she have to lose? They were hardly going to be bumping into each other on opposite sides of the Channel after this trip. Once she might have been tempted to tell him in order to deflate some of his arrogance—but now she wanted to tell him for a very different reason. Because she was a friend, and she cared.

'Okay, then, I'll tell you,' she said. 'Yours seems a rich life only in the most superficial of ways. Like you're being carried along on a wave of luxury and not really connecting properly with people. Like money matters and nothing else.' Her voice tailed off and she gave a little shrug. 'That's all.'

'That's *all*? You demolish my very existence and say *that's all*? You think your own life is so great, do you, Laura?'

'Of course I don't!' she burst out frustratedly. 'I *knew* this would happen. I'm not here to sit in judgement on you, Xavier—but you did ask.'

Yes, he had—and she had told him, with breathtaking honesty. He could not think of a single other person in the world who would have had the courage to do that. Was some of what she said right? he wondered.

'Why did you take this job?' he asked suddenly.

Laura stared hard at her fingers, which had acquired a faint tan from the Kharastan sun. How much more of her honesty did he want—and how much of her story did she want to tell? But friendship—true friendship—wasn't one-sided.

'Oh, the usual. A man. Josh.'

'And you were in love with this *Josh*?' he said, scarcely believing that *he* should ask such a question. He was sounding like one of those men he had always despised. Like one of those jealous fools who were bothered by other men.

'I *thought* I was in love with him,' Laura answered. 'But that may just have been my own justification for sleeping with him.'

In one sentence she had exposed her relative innocence, and Xavier wondered if she was aware that her faint shudder had told him everything he needed to know about her physical relationship with this other man.

Was that what made him suddenly feel so guilty—the fact that he had judged her so harshly and made those false allegations against her?

'But, no, on reflection—it wasn't love,' she said, after a bit more thought. 'He dazzled me—but he turned out to be shallow. He just seemed so *exciting*. I'd worked hard to get my law degree—taken so many jobs during the holidays because money was tight—that I'd never really stopped to have fun.' She gave a rueful smile. 'And while Josh had the worst CV I've ever seen—he certainly knew how to have fun.'

'What happened?'

Laura shrugged. 'We bought a house in joint names, but our contribution to its upkeep was—how shall I put this?—unequal. Josh still wasn't working, and I was putting in more and more hours just to pay the bills. When he started playing around I knew I wanted him out of my life—but I wasn't prepared to lose the home I'd worked so hard for. I'd spent my childhood in a series of rented flats, and I couldn't bear to go back to that way of life. And so when my boss suggested that the royal household of Kharastan needed a discreet lawyer urgently—well, it seemed like the answer to all my prayers. I'd be able to buy Josh out and be free.'

'Free?' he said thoughtfully.

'That's right.'

There was silence while Xavier thought about what

she had told him. He wanted to reach out to touch her, to run his hands over the slippery red satin of her hair. But he had no right to do that.

For, while his lips might curve with disdain at the antics of her ex-boyfriend, in a way, wasn't he, Xavier, just as guilty of using her, of trying to impose *his* wishes on her as Josh had been?

He had spoken to Malik and asked—no, *demanded* that Laura stay here. But that had been when he'd imagined she would change her mind about sleeping with him again. Because it was inconceivable that any women could not be seduced, or bent to his will.

But her quiet resolve had been firm, and suddenly Xavier was appalled at his own behaviour. His determination to succeed—or rather to have exactly what it was he wanted—had spilled over from his professional into his personal life. And he didn't like it.

They were almost back at the Blue Palace—he could see the wide sweep of road which led to the main gates and the pluming fountains beyond. He knew what he needed to do.

'I won't hold you here any longer against your will, Laura,' he said heavily. 'I should never have done so in the first place. You are free to leave at any time. You can go home.'

Laura had been staring out of the window at a bird with orange plumage, nestling in among the flowers on some beautiful unknown tree, and his words hit her like a bucket of cold water on a hot day. Carefully, she composed her face into some sort of smile, hoping against hope that it masked her dismay.

'Home?' she questioned, as if it was a word in Kharastani that she was hoping to learn before they arrived back at the Palace.

He nodded. 'Just as soon as you like. I'll speak to Malik.'

Here was the freedom she had convinced herself she wanted. Yet wasn't it ironic that you could tell yourself you wanted something over and over again and yet, when it finally came, it left you feeling as if someone had blasted a great hole in the centre of your heart?

CHAPTER TWELVE

'THE Sheikh wishes to see you.'

Laura looked up from her case—which, to Sidonia's horror, she had insisted on packing herself—to see Xavier standing framed in the doorway of her bedroom. His black eyes were watchful as she folded an exquisite silk-satin evening gown, and she wondered if she'd ever get the chance to wear it again. But at least focussing on practical considerations like that stopped her from thinking how much she was going to miss the Frenchman.

'He wants to see me? What for?'

'Mind-reading has never been a particular skill of mine,' he drawled 'Why don't you ask him yourself? I'm to take you there.'

'Not Malik?'

'Apparently not.'

Their eyes met. Laura wanted to tell him that she was going to miss him, that she wished now she'd opted for one more taste of the joy she'd found in his arms. She wanted to tell him that she longed to stay here, in this enchanted paradise—with him. But he was letting her go, and she must do just that. Laura was headed home. Alone.

But I *am* going to miss you, she thought sadly as she stared into the soft ebony blaze of his eyes.

Her hand flew up to brush away a stray strand of hair from her cheek before she met the Sheikh. 'Do I look okay?'

He knew that this was not the disingenuous snaring of a compliment. He knew that the boyfriend who had tried to rip her off had destroyed a lot of her confidence. But in her simple linen dress, with her red hair tied back in a ribbon, she looked good enough to... He felt a nerve work in his cheek. 'You look beautiful.'

Laura supposed it would be churlish to tell him that she wanted his approval, but not with such a high rating—because when he used words like *beautiful* it made her start wanting what she had told herself she couldn't have. And she could *never* have Xavier in the way she would most like him—as a proper boyfriend she could do normal relationship stuff with.

She had thought that friendship was the answer, but in that it seemed she had been wrong—because friendship was almost as perilous as sex in making you feel close to a man. Well, maybe more so. The sex she'd had with Xavier had been the best sex of her life, and even though she had laughably little to compare it with she knew deep down that she would never have another lover like him.

But their friendship felt special. Different. As she suspected it was. He was letting her come closer than he would normally let *anyone* come—because of the bizarre circumstances of their being literally thrown together.

Well, today it was coming to an end, and while Laura was trying to tell herself that it was a job well done, inside her heart was heavy. But as she slipped out into the wide marbled corridor she thought that she hid it rather well.

'I wonder what he wants?' she mused, as Xavier fell into step beside her. 'You know—it's actually the first time that I'll have met him. I've always dealt with Malik before.'

'Presumably he wants to say goodbye.'

'I hate goodbyes,' said Laura fiercely.

Usually Xavier didn't. Usually he relished closure—the chance to cut ties, to move on and start anew. But today didn't feel anything like that. Laura was leaving, and he was not experiencing his habitual release.

'Have you…decided how long you're going to stay?' asked Laura.

'No.' He gave a short laugh. 'For the first time in my life I'm not certain of anything. I'm lucky enough to have the choice—many men are locked into jobs they cannot take leave from.'

'You *are* lucky,' she echoed.

'Yes, I am,' he agreed quietly. But when had he last *counted* his blessings? Got off the speeding train which was his life in order to enjoy some of the benefits he'd worked so hard for? Look at the way Laura's face had lit up when she'd spoken about buying Josh out and getting her own house and independence. Had prosperity made this former Paris urchin spoilt and unappreciative?

'Maybe he'll make you his heir,' said Laura. 'What then?'

'I doubt it,' said Xavier, with a frown. 'And don't you know that you should never plan for the future?'

Laura didn't want to think about the future, so she concentrated on looking at some of the ancient paintings of Kharastan which lined the high walls.

Their echoing footsteps took them along more wide marble corridors, and Laura thought about the strange contradiction of the Palace. How exquisite and beautiful it was—while outside lay the wild and unremitting desert, like a hungry beast just waiting to reclaim the land.

Did the Sheikh think of things like that as he grew ever older? she wondered. Was it a cultural imperative for him to hand the reins over to his kith and kin—and was he now about to pass on such a weighty responsibility to Xavier? Because if he didn't make his son his heir, then what would happen to Kharastan, and who would rule it?

She stole a look at his hard, set profile and he looked down at her, his eyes momentarily softening in a way they rarely did.

'You look sad,' she observed.

He sighed. She was so perceptive. And you're going to miss *that*, aren't you? taunted a voice inside his head.

'I am—a little. It feels strange that, having found him,

I shall soon go back to my own life in Paris. Life is so unpredictable that this might be the last time I ever see him.'

'It might,' she agreed. 'But at least you've had this heaven-sent opportunity to get to know him.

They were outside the Sheikh's apartments now, and the ornate doors opened and Malik appeared, his eyes black-chipped and hard.

'He will see you both now,' he said curtly.

The light in the Sheikh's glorious golden room was muted and soft, and the air was cooled by some unseen fan and scented with the faint perfume of fresh flowers.

Aware of Malik behind her and Xavier by her side, Laura suddenly felt like an outsider. Why did Kharastan's ruler want to see her? she wondered.

'Approach,' came the soft command from a divan, and Laura suddenly forgot all her misgivings as she realised what a great honour was being afforded to her. As she drew close to the old man she sank instinctively into a deep curtsey—without having been aware that she even knew how to perform such a graceful gesture of homage. There she stayed, her eyes downcast, until she felt his hand on the top of her head.

'Arise,' he husked. 'Thank you for bringing my son to me, Miss Cottingham.'

'It was my…pleasure,' said Laura, her heart beating fast with nerves.

Xavier had moved forward, too—and Malik was indicating that she should sit on a low stool beside the Sheikh.

Laura didn't know what she had been expecting.

Golden robes denoted his privileged position, and the Sheikh was old, yes—but he carried with him the indefinable aura of power. And Xavier was right—his eyes were as memorably black as his son's. He sat up—as if the sight of the three of them had in some magical way revitalised him. A male servant appeared, to offer him a drink from a goblet inlaid with precious stones, but the Sheikh waved him away.

'Xavier, you are my son,' said the Sheikh. 'And I am granting you the freedom of Kharastan. Designated lands and great wealth will be made available to you in this, your country.'

'I thank you, but I have no need of your gift,' said Xavier proudly. 'And that is not the reason I came.'

The Sheikh nodded approvingly. 'I know and understand that—for you have made your own wealth in life. You have succeeded as I would have expected. These gifts are not made because of their financial worth—but because they are yours by birthright. The past can never be rewritten, my son—only the future is ours to forge, and yours lies ahead of you. You must go where destiny takes you—but you will always have a place and a home here, as one of the Sheikh's sons,' he finished quietly.

There was silence for a moment, and Laura was so awestruck that she wasn't really listening with her usual sharp and analytical lawyer's ear.

But Xavier was. And his eyes narrowed as one phrase leapt into his mind and fastened itself there, like a leech.

'*One* of the Sheikh's sons?' he repeated.

Laura saw the look which passed between Malik and the Sheikh.

'There is another son?' Xavier demanded hoarsely. 'I have a...*brother*?'

'You have a half-brother,' said the Sheikh carefully. 'Unlike you, he is Italian, and lives in the land of his birth.'

Xavier stared at the Sheikh. *'Why?'* he whispered.

It was a question which could have been interpreted in many ways, Laura thought—though the Sheikh seemed to know exactly what it was that Xavier demanded to know with that single word.

The Sheikh glanced around the room, nodding to dismiss the servants so that only he, Xavier and Malik remained. And Laura of course—who was half expecting them to ask her to leave as well. But they did not.

'Because I made a great dynastic marriage at a time of civil unrest in Kharastan, and my people dearly loved my wife. As did I,' he added softly. 'It was a successful marriage on many levels except on one—I never had a child with her.'

'You just went round procreating throughout Europe, did you?' accused Xavier hotly.

Laura saw Malik scowl and half rise, but the Sheikh stayed him by lifting his hand.

'You have a right to express your anger, Xavier—but, as I have already told you, we cannot rewrite the past, and we prepare for our future only by how we behave now, in the present.'

For a moment there was silence, and then eventually

Xavier spoke, but even to his own ears his voice sounded strange and disconnected. He had a *brother*! 'And what of this half-brother of mine?'

The Sheikh stared at him. 'Would you like to meet him? We could send Miss Cottingham to Naples, to persuade him to come to Kharastan.'

Xavier's fingers curled into two tight fists and his face darkened as he looked at Malik and Laura.

'Leave us!' he commanded them all. 'Please leave me alone with the Sheikh, my father.'

It was, Laura noted, the first time Xavier had acknowledged the relationship aloud. She also noted Malik's questioning glance at the Sheikh, but the old man nodded, so he rose to his feet and so did Laura, before she followed him out.

As she went back to her room, she *did* feel like an outsider, and strangely overcome—by all that she had seen and learnt, by the sense that an opportunity lay ahead for her to go on another great adventure to bring back son number two. But the feeling which most overwhelmed her was one of immense sadness.

Because you have to say goodbye to the man who has ensnared your heart? Is that why you'll even *consider* going to Italy, to deal with the half-brother, knowing that it will somehow keep you in Xavier's life? Is that what you want?

She had finished packing and was standing by the window, watching one of the guards on horseback as he clip-clopped his way around the grounds, when she heard footsteps behind her. She turned round to see Xavier standing there.

His face was like stone—cold and unyielding. Yet his eyes glittered suspiciously bright, and Laura was more surprised by that than by anything. Had Xavier actually shed *tears*?

'What did you say to him?' she questioned huskily.

He looked at her and his eyes cleared—as if he were just emerging from a forest into a bright open space, but as if the shadows of that dark place he had visited would never quite leave him.

'We said things which shall forever remain between father and son,' he said gravely.

She saw the pain in his eyes and heard the dignity in his voice, and in that single moment her heart turned over and she knew that she loved him. She knew too that it was a non-starter—but as long as she could hold onto that fact then she'd be okay. Because what had Xavier once said to her? Regret wasn't part of his agenda? Well, it wouldn't be part of hers, either.

Let him go, she told herself. Don't be like the blonde who flounced out of his office the first time you met him. There are streams of women like her in his past, and no doubt streams of them waiting in his future. So replicate *his* dignity as you say goodbye.

'You'll stay here?' she asked.

'For a while. Laura—'

Her head jerked up, her eyes wide. 'What?' she questioned breathlessly.

'You won't take the job of going to find Giovanni, will you?'

The hope in her heart sank like a stone in a muddy pond, gone without trace. 'Is that a request or an order, Xavier?'

There was a heartbeat of a pause. 'It can be either,' he said steadily.

'You're *forbidding* it—even though the Sheikh himself asked me?'

'I can override that request if it does not please me,' he said stubbornly.

'If it does not please me?' she choked. 'What's the matter, Xavier? Do you think I'll end up in bed with your half-brother?'

'Stop it!' he snapped, as unwanted erotic images swam darkly into his mind. That kind of turmoil was the last thing he needed at the moment. 'Very well! Take the damned job if you wish to!'

'Thank you—I will!'

'You will?'

'I'll give it some thought.'

He scowled. 'Have you finished packing? Because I'm going to take you to the airport.'

And witness her breaking down into tears? His angry words washed over her and brought Laura to her senses. What of her hard-won self-respect and the dignity with which she wished to be remembered?

'Thanks, but no thanks, Xavier,' she said quietly. 'I'd

prefer it if one of the drivers took me. And now, if you wouldn't mind leaving, I have a plane to catch and I need to change first.'

CHAPTER THIRTEEN

LAURA arrived home in Dolchester and couldn't quite shake off a feeling of disorientation which didn't feel like jet-lag.

It wasn't just the fact that it was raining—a soft summer rain which washed all the dust off the flowers—because the rain felt quite soothing after the heat of the desert. Or the fact that the boiler had stopped working and she had no water for a bath.

It was...

Xavier.

Of course it was Xavier.

But, in a funny way, being back in the little market town helped. Just looking around at it and contrasting it with what she had left behind in Kharastan was enough to help her try to see things clearly. What was the point of shedding tears for something so unob-tainable as the Sheikh's son?

Even if he hadn't been half-royal he was still totally wrong for her. And as the familiar surroundings re-established themselves on Laura's consciousness they made a mockery of her heart's desire.

Could she ever really imagine Xavier here? Stooping his tall body to get in the front door, knocking his dark head on one of the beams which hung so low in the sitting room? Or perhaps going down to the local pub with her and ordering a pint of lager? Maybe even braving the local shops, where you had to be prepared to divulge your life history if you wanted to purchase so much as a bunch of bananas?

Of course she could switch it around the other way. Laura in Paris! Laura sticking out like a sore thumb as she marched up the smart Avenue Georges V, or dined in the top-rate restaurants which Xavier no doubt frequented all the time. Laura with her schoolgirl French, trying to make herself understood in the *boulangerie*.

She had put all her Kharastan clothes in a wardrobe in the spare bedroom, because they seemed all wrong here. Until some enterprising soul opened one of those Middle-Eastern restaurants which were taking London by storm she could hardly wear them—could hardly walk into the local bank with embroidered jade-green silk brushing the floor, could she?

On the plus side, she had bought Josh out with her generous settlement from Kharastan, and Laura wouldn't have been human if that hadn't given her satisfaction. He had boasted of sleeping with one of the barmaids at the Black Dog pub, but as soon as Laura had shown a bit of financial clout he'd seemed to find *her* desirable.

'Get *off*, Josh!' she had said, when he'd made an unexpected lunge at her just after he had signed the papers transferring the cottage into her name. 'I'm just not interested any more.'

'What's got into you?' he'd sneered.

Laura had resisted the urge to tell him that a real man had made her realise just what she'd been missing for so long, because she was more mature than that. Xavier was her own special secret.

And you know that Josh will mock you if he finds out that it's over!

But she'd blocked that thought and closed the door behind Josh once and for all. She wasn't going to think negatively. Seeing Zahir nearing the end of his life had made her realise how precious time was, and she was going to treasure every second of it. She couldn't have Xavier, no—but that did not mean she was going to waste her life crying pointless tears about him. She would treasure the memories—put them in the back of her mind to be brought out on rainy days and Sundays.

It was night-times she found most difficult—that was when the stupid yearnings became hardest to push away. Like wishing she had been his lover for the whole time they'd been there—because what had she gained by resisting him, other than pride and an aching sense of what she had missed? And pride made a lonely bedfellow.

Laura told herself that it was natural to cry, and cathartic, too—even if some nights she had to bury her face in the pillow so that she wouldn't have to listen to the sound of her own broken sobs echoing round the room.

She had been back a month, and had just about accepted that she wasn't going to hear any more from Kharastan after writing to Malik declining the offer to go to Naples, saying that she really could not take any more time off work. It was a sunny Saturday morning, and she paused in the act of ladling strawberry jam onto a slice of toast as she heard a loud knock at the door.

The postman? she wondered as she opened it—and froze when she saw the man on her doorstep, dark and golden, glowing and vibrant, and looking just too good to be true against the backdrop of her tiny front garden.

Laura clutched the door-handle and stared at him, as if he might be a figment of her aching imagination and might suddenly just disappear. Yet after their last fraught meeting surely she should have felt anger, or indignation? So why was she experiencing a wild, fluttering kind of joy—tempered only by uncertainty?

'Xavier!' She almost put her hand out—as if to see if it was an apparition. 'Is it really you?' she whispered.

'You think I have a double?'

God, no. They'd broken the mould when they made *him*. 'What…?' She swallowed. For heaven's sake, Laura—just pull yourself together. 'What are you doing here?'

His lips curved into a quizzical smile. 'English hospitality leaves much to be desired,' he murmured. 'Aren't you going to ask me in?'

'Yes. Of course. Come in. Mind your— Oh, Xavier! Have you hurt your head?'

'*Non*,' he murmured, rubbing it with a grimace and wondering if England had once been populated by a race of pygmies.

Laura smoothed her hands down over her hair, which was hanging loose to her waist, and wished that someone could wave a magic wand and transform her. She wore a pair of old jeans, a T-shirt she'd had since college which said *Lawyers Do It In Briefs!*, and not a scrap of make-up on her face.

'Why didn't you tell me you were coming?' she demanded. 'At least I could have dressed up.'

'I didn't want you to dress up. I like the way you look,' he said slowly, as his eyes drank her in. 'You look…different.'

He looked different, too—Laura realised. In black jeans which emphasised the long, muscular thrust of his thighs and a dark leather jacket. And he was taking the jacket off without being asked, she thought, as a wave of dizziness washed over her. Did that mean he was staying? Well, he hadn't come all the way from Kharastan—or even Paris—just to turn around and go back again! But staying for how long? And did she have the guts to ask him what he was here for?

'Would you like coffee?' she babbled frantically. 'It's

not real coffee, because I only buy that when I'm having a dinner party.'

'Not *real* coffee?' he asked, genuinely perplexed for a moment. 'You mean it's…pretend?'

'It's instant.' Now he would see for himself how the real Laura Cottingham was—nothing but an unsophisticated small-town lawyer, who wore unsophisticated small-town clothes and drank instant coffee from a jar most of the time!

Xavier shook his head slightly. This wasn't going as he had planned, and for the first time in his life he felt the shimmer of doubt.

The air was very still for a moment as he looked at her.

'You didn't take the job?'

She shrugged. Had she really entertained the notion for more than a nano-second that she would track down Xavier's half-brother? 'No, I decided it wasn't really such a good idea.'

In that they were in perfect accord. Xavier expelled a long breath of relief, but he was still no closer to obtaining his heart's desire.

'Would you like to come to Paris instead?'

Laura's heart missed another beat. 'Paris?' she repeated cautiously. 'What for?'

Their eyes met.

'What do you think?'

'I don't know,' she whispered. *Ask him.* 'Why are you here, Xavier?'

'Because something has happened to me—something that you have done to me,' he said. 'Something I cannot reverse, although in truth I have tried—*mais oui*, I have tried! I thought the confusion in my head was because I'd discovered my father—but soon I saw that this was not so.'

'You're not making any sense.'

'You think I don't know this?' He shook his head as if he were clearing his thoughts—or marvelling that he should have them in the first place. 'I realised that the things you said to me were true—that I cared more for *things* than I did about people. And I don't want to live that way any more. You made me look at things differently, Laura,' he continued, when still she said nothing. 'You made me want more of what I had with you—something I'd spent my whole life running away from.'

'And what was that?'

There was a pause. 'Emotion,' he said eventually. '*Oui.*' And, seeing her look of amazement, he shrugged and gave her a look which was the closest Xavier de Maistre had ever come to being helpless.

'I kept remembering your face,' he said, in a voice which was almost dreamy. 'When something happened which amused or angered me I found myself wanting to tell you. I would lie in bed at night, reliving the moments I had with you—both erotic and tender moments, and not nearly enough of them.'

His eyes were intensely black as he stared at her, the blackest she had ever seen them.

SHARON KENDRICK   179

'It's driving me crazy. *You're* driving me crazy.' He swallowed. 'I've missed you, Laura.'

Her heart lurched with excitement, hope, fear. 'Missed? Past tense?'

'Always the lawyer's precison with words,' he mocked. 'Okay, I miss you. I *miss* you,' he repeated, slowly and deliberately. 'How's that?'

Laura could feel the swirl of uncertainty, and she was afraid that he would see her terrible need, her desire—all the things which made her feel vulnerable around him—and be turned off by them. Was she grown-up enough to handle an affair, which was presumably what he was offering?

'I want to be with you,' he continued, and then his face became dark with passion, intent with something else. '*Je t'aime*,' he said softly, and then added, 'I love you.'

Laura knew what it meant—everyone who had ever learnt French at school knew what it meant. And if someone had asked her what she wanted most in the world, then Xavier had just given it to her in those three words. But she was frightened. Terrified, in fact. She was like a unsure skater who had been told it was safe to go on the ice—yet some instinct of self-preservation made her want to test how solid it was.

'How many other women have you said that to?'

'None. Only you.'

'We haven't known each other for very long.'

'I know that.'

'And we've never been together in normal circumstances.'

'I know that, too.'

'Well, what if it won't work?' she said desperately.

For the first time he touched her—reaching out to brush away a stray lock of hair which had fallen onto her pale cheek. 'What if? What if?' he murmured softly. 'Why don't you come to Paris and we'll make sure it works? Together.'

The Laura of a few months ago would have baulked at the suggestion of throwing caution to the wind and taking a step into the unknown. But that had been before Kharastan—an experience which had affected her profoundly and for which, ultimately, she had the cheating Josh to thank. And Xavier too, of course. In Kharastan he had wanted her on his terms, but she had resisted going for the easy fix. She had grown a new self-respect—and was no longer victim or coward.

She stared at him and then pointed to her old clothes, her gesture taking in the sweet little cottage room, which was a million light years away from his sophisticated urban style.

'But this is the real me,' she said. 'That expensively clad woman you met doesn't exist.'

He laughed softly as he shook his dark head, and his fingertips traced her eyelids, her nose, her lips, and then came to rest at last over her pounding heart.

'No,' he demurred. '*This* is the real you. The woman who has touched my heart and body and soul. The woman who made me look at myself, who made me think things I sometimes cared not to think. The woman who haunts my waking and sleeping hours and the woman I long to kiss once more.'

'Then kiss me,' she breathed.

He took her into his arms and groaned as he brushed his mouth over hers.

'Where's the bedroom?' he growled, after a few frantic moments.

'You won't need a route map,' she gasped. 'There's only two, and it's upstairs. Come with me.'

He had to dip his head again to enter the miniature bedroom with a bed which was a little small for his taste, but he laid her down on it, pulling off her underwear, throwing it aside with the rest of his own clothes with none of his usual teasing restraint, uncaring. In fact, uncaring of anything other than the urgent need to join with her completely.

It was only a brief interlude of sanity which reminded him to protect himself—and *that* near-slip dazed him, too, for it was always at the very top of his agenda.

Laura sobbed as he entered her, and he licked her tears away with his tongue as he slicked in and out of her. She whimpered with pleasure, wanting to hold onto it—to cherish the feeling and the movement and the moment—but she was fighting a losing battle.

'Oh, Xavier!' she cried, and tightened her arms around him as if she would never let him go.

He had known it was about to happen—had observed

it from the rosy flowering at her breasts—and he knew he wanted to be with her, the same journey at the same time, leading to the same place. He had never had simultaneous orgasm before—the icy control at the very core of his being had never wanted to make himself quite that powerless—but this time he craved it with a hunger which overwhelmed him.

Xavier let go, letting his orgasm take him up, and he followed it—swooping upwards just like the falcon who chased the lure. For a moment he felt at one with her—just as the sound of the wind seemed part of the desert itself—which was part of him.

Never had his peak lasted for so long, and never had the sweet spasms taken so long to subside—so that for a moment he felt as though he had wandered into some unknown place of such enchanting beauty that it could not possibly exist. A place a little like Kharastan? Yes!

When he looked into her eyes he could see the glimmer of another tear on her cheek, and he wiped it away with the tip of a gentle fingertip.

Laura bit her lip. 'Oh, Xavier,' she gulped. 'I love you so much.'

He looked down into her emerald eyes, so clear and bright, shining with an emotion she no longer had to hide, and his heart turned over with love. 'I know that, too,' he said softly.

EPILOGUE

DESERT WEDDING FOR *SHEIKH'S ILLEGITIMATE SON!*

THE press had gone wild—it was the biggest international story in years. Xavier's Parisian apartment was staked out by representatives from the media, so that in the end he and Laura had to employ a firm of heavies to keep them away.

They had tried to keep the wedding and its location a secret, but inevitably—with an event of this magnitude—it was bound to leak out. Kharastan was set to have its first big royal wedding in decades. Its people had taken the Sheikh's son to their hearts, and they adored his beautiful bride-to-be, with her sunset-coloured hair and eyes the colour of the forests.

'Did that surprise you?' Laura asked Xavier curiously one morning. 'That they should so quickly accept you, in view of the strange circumstances of your birth?

Xavier shook his head. 'During the month I spent

there after you had gone they got to know me a little, and as time goes by they shall know me better still.' He smiled. 'But their approval has been my father's reward for his loyalty to his late wife, and for the just and fair way he has ruled the land.'

They were lying in bed, in the huge apartment whose windows reflected the shimmering light of the Seine, and every so often Laura would hold up her hand to admire the whacking great square-cut emerald engagement ring which glittered on her finger—and which Xavier said mirrored perfectly the colour of her eyes.

In a month's time—when the plans were ready to be finalised—the two of them would fly out to Kharastan for their wedding, and a honeymoon in the countryside afterwards.

She turned to him and stroked the bare flesh of his shoulder thoughtfully. 'Is this all happening too quickly, do you think?'

'No. Do you?'

She shook her head and smiled. 'I want to be your wife, Xavier. More than anything else in the world.'

He smiled, touched his fingertips to her lips. 'Well, then—I want that, too. I want to make you legally mine—to bind you to me for the rest of our days.'

Laura shivered as she heard his masterful intent and snuggled up to him, thinking that life couldn't get much more perfect than this.

She had gone to Paris with the intention of finding

her own apartment and her own job—but work had quickly come her way, courtesy of Xavier, and surely only a stubborn fool would have turned it away?

She had tried looking for an apartment on her own, too—and, interestingly, the area she'd liked best was the Marais, where Xavier had grown up which was now one of the smartest areas in the city! But then she'd realised that she didn't want to spend nights apart, and neither did he. She wanted to be there in the mornings, and there in the evenings, and at all the other times in between. The two of them together seemed almost pre-ordained—as if anything else but Xavier and Laura as a couple was unimaginable. And when Xavier had asked her to marry him one sunlit morning as they walked out to buy baguettes for breakfast, she had burst into tears of joy.

It *was* soon—she knew that and he knew that—but there was a reason for that, unspoken but understood. His father was still alive, and Xavier wanted to show the Sheikh that there was going to be continuity in his illegitimate son's life. That he was marrying someone the Sheikh had met, and of whom he approved.

At least the question of inheriting the kingdom was not an issue—Giovanni was older than Xavier.

'Thank heavens for that,' Laura had murmured with genuine gratitude when she'd found out. 'I wonder if he's going to reply to the invitation to our wedding? I really hope he does come—I'd like to meet him.'

At the mention of Giovanni, his half-brother, Xavier

felt his heart leap with a joy tempered by trepidation. But Laura had taught him not to fear his feelings any more—to let them in and just go with the flow.

She had taught him that, and so much else. But the most important thing she had taught him was how to love.

0307/WOMAN'S WEEKLY/AD

The weekly magazine you'll use every day!

Woman's Weekly ®

Why not
take out a subscription
for your Woman's Weekly?
Call 0845 676 7778
quoting 20A, or visit
www.ipcsubs.co.uk/iwka

On sale every Wednesday

●Cookery ●Health ●Fiction
●Fashion ●Home ●Beauty
●Gardening ●Real-life stories,
and much, much more

0307/01a

MILLS & BOON®

Modern
romance™

THE MARRIAGE POSSESSION by *Helen Bianchin*
Lisane Deveraux is a successful lawyer by day and Zac
Winstone's passionate mistress by night. But a surprise
pregnancy changes everything and Zac proposes. Lisane
prepares herself for a life as Zac's trophy wife in public
and his mistress in private... His heart will never be part
of the deal...

THE SHEIKH'S UNWILLING WIFE
by *Sharon Kendrick*
Five years ago Alexa walked out on her marriage, taking
with her a precious secret. Giovanni is the son of a
powerful desert ruler and he's determined that Alexa
should resume her position as his wife. But how will he
react when he discovers he has a son...?

THE ITALIAN'S INEXPERIENCED MISTRESS
by *Lynne Graham*
When Angelo set out to get revenge, innocent Gwenna
Hamilton reluctantly accepted the Italian tycoon's offer
to pay for her father's freedom with her body. Gwenna
thought Angelo would tire of her and her inexperience
quickly. But he wanted more than just one night...

THE SICILIAN'S VIRGIN BRIDE by *Sarah Morgan*
All billionaire Rocco Castellani had wished for was a
biddable wife – instead Francesca had gone before the
first dance at their wedding! But Rocco has tracked her
down... He was cheated out of his wedding night – and
nothing is going to stop him claiming his virgin bride...

On sale 6th April 2007

Available at WHSmith, Tesco, ASDA, and all good bookshops
www.millsandboon.co.uk

MILLS & BOON®

0307/01b

Modern
romance™

THE RICH MAN'S BRIDE by *Catherine George*

Ever since Anna Morton was snubbed by wealthy Ryder
Wyndham she's kept her distance from the man she once
worshipped. Then Anna is forced to live with Ryder, and
tension turns to temptation… Anna has no plans to settle
down – but Ryder is determined that she will be his lady-
of-the-manor bride!

WIFE BY CONTRACT, MISTRESS BY DEMAND
by *Carole Mortimer*

Gabriella Benito fell for her wealthy stepbrother Rufus
Gresham the day she set eyes on him. But Rufus believed
she was a gold digger… Then they are obliged to marry
to secure their inheritances. At the wedding, Rufus kisses
Gabriella passionately – is he using their marriage as an
excuse to get her in his bed…?

WIFE BY APPROVAL by *Lee Wilkinson*

Richard Anders is heir to the sumptuous Castle Anders
and needs gorgeous Valentina to secure his birthright.
Valentina is swept off her feet by this handsome
gentleman. Soon she's given him her innocence in the
bedroom, she's given him her word at the altar, but when
she learns the truth will she give Richard her heart?

THE SHEIKH'S RANSOMED BRIDE by *Annie West*

Kidnapped by rebels, Belle Winters is rescued by Rafiq
al Akhtar, Sovereign Prince of the desert kingdom of
Q'aroum. Whisked away to his exotic palace, she learns
that Rafiq expects her to show her gratitude by marrying
him! Rafiq intends her to carry out her royal duties both
in public – and in private…

On sale 6th April 2007

Available at WHSmith, Tesco, ASDA, and all good bookshops

www.millsandboon.co.uk

0307/05a

MILLS & BOON®

In April 2007 Mills & Boon present two
classic collections, each featuring three
wonderful romances by three of our
bestselling authors…

Mediterranean Weddings

Featuring
A Mediterranean Marriage by Lynne Graham
The Greek's Virgin Bride by Julia James
The Italian Prince's Proposal by Susan Stephens

On sale 6th April 2007

Available at WHSmith, Tesco, ASDA, and all good bookshops
www.millsandboon.co.uk

0307/05b

MILLS & BOON®

Whose Baby?

Featuring
With This Baby… by Caroline Anderson
The Italian's Baby by Lucy Gordon
Assignment: Baby by Jessica Hart

Don't miss out on these superb stories!

On sale 6th April 2007

Available at WHSmith, Tesco, ASDA, and all good bookshops
www.millsandboon.co.uk

FREE!

4 Books
and a surprise gift!

We would like to take this opportunity to thank you for reading this Mills & Boon® book by offering you the chance to take FOUR more specially selected titles from the Modern Romance™ series absolutely FREE! We're also making this offer to introduce you to the benefits of the Mills & Boon® Reader Service™—

- ★ **FREE home delivery**
- ★ **FREE gifts and competitions**
- ★ **FREE monthly Newsletter**
- ★ **Exclusive Reader Service offers**
- ★ **Books available before they're in the shops**

Accepting these FREE books and gift places you under no obligation to buy, you may cancel at any time, even after receiving your free shipment. Simply complete your details below and return the entire page to the address below. You don't even need a stamp!

YES! Please send me 4 free Modern Romance books and a surprise gift. I understand that unless you hear from me, I will receive 6 superb new titles every month for just £2.89 each, postage and packing free. I am under no obligation to purchase any books and may cancel my subscription at any time. The free books and gift will be mine to keep in any case.

P7ZEF

Ms/Mrs/Miss/Mr ....Initials ....

BLOCK CAPITALS PLEASE

Surname ....

Address ....

....

....Postcode ....

Send this whole page to:
UK: FREEPOST CN81, Croydon, CR9 3WZ

Offer valid in UK only and is not available to current Mills & Boon® Reader Service™ subscribers to this series. Overseas and Eire please write for details. We reserve the right to refuse an application and applicants must be aged 18 years or over. Only one application per household. Terms and prices subject to change without notice. Offer expires 31st May 2007. As a result of this application, you may receive offers from Harlequin Mills & Boon and other carefully selected companies. If you would prefer not to share in this opportunity please write to The Data Manager, PO Box 676, Richmond, TW9 1WU.

Mills & Boon® is a registered trademark owned by Harlequin Mills & Boon Limited.
Modern Romance™ is being used as a trademark. The Mills & Boon® Reader Service™ is being used as a trademark.